***The heartw...*** *
***pinned Cupid with a glare.***

"Would you like to tell me what that was all about?" he demanded. "Do you know who that was? That was my mail-order bride, and you just gave her away to someone else!" he raged.

Cupid gasped. This had never happened before. She brought people love, not disappointment. "Well," she said, "she wasn't right for you anyway."

"And just who are you to interfere in my love life? Cupid?" he snapped.

Cupid tipped her plastic name tag at him. *Cupid Jones, Postmistress, Valentine, Kansas.*

Burke took her in—every adorable, vexing inch of her. But quickly his ire resurfaced. Cupid Jones had shredded his carefully laid plans. He wanted a wife on his remote ranch but didn't have the time or inclination to find the perfect match. This arranged marriage was a practical solution.

He squared his broad shoulders, purposely allowing a bit of intimidation to creep into his stance. "Well, Miss Cupid," he drawled, "you gave away my bride, so you can just find me another."

Dear Reader,

In the spirit of Valentine's Day, we have some wonderful stories for you this February from Silhouette Romance to guarantee that every day is filled with love and tenderness.

DeAnna Talcott puts a fresh spin on the tale of Cupid, who finally meets her match in *Cupid Jones Gets Married* (#1646), the latest in the popular SOULMATES series. And Carla Cassidy has been working overtime with her incredibly innovative, incredibly fun duo, *What if I'm Pregnant...?* (#1644) and *If the Stick Turns Pink...* (#1645), about the promise of love a baby could bring to two special couples!

Then Elizabeth Harbison takes us on a fairy-tale adventure in *Princess Takes a Holiday* (#1643). A glamour-weary royal who hides her identity meets the man of her dreams when her car breaks down in a small North Carolina town. In *Dude Ranch Bride* (#1642), Madeline Baker brings us strong, sexy Lakota Ethan Stormwalker, whose ex-flame shows up at his ranch in a wedding gown—without a groom! And in Donna Clayton's *Thunder in the Night* (#1647), the third in THE THUNDER CLAN family saga, a single act of kindness changes Conner Thunder's life forever....

Be sure to come back next month for more emotion-filled love stories from Silhouette Romance. Happy reading!

*Mary-Theresa Hussey*

Mary-Theresa Hussey
Senior Editor

Please address questions and book requests to:
Silhouette Reader Service
U.S.: 3010 Walden Ave., P.O. Box 1325, Buffalo, NY 14269
Canadian: P.O. Box 609, Fort Erie, Ont. L2A 5X3

# Cupid Jones
# Gets Married

## DeAnna TALCOTT

SILHOUETTE *Romance*

Published by Silhouette Books

America's Publisher of Contemporary Romance

SILHOUETTE BOOKS

ISBN 0-373-19646-6

CUPID JONES GETS MARRIED

Visit Silhouette at www.eHarlequin.com

**Printed in U.S.A.**

**Books by DeAnna Talcott**

Silhouette Romance

*The Cowboy and the Christmas Tree* #1125
*The Bachelor and the Bassinet,* #1189
*To Wed Again?* #1206
*The Triplet's Wedding Wish* #1370
*Marrying for a Mom* #1543
*The Nanny & Her Scrooge* #1568
*Her Last Chance* #1628
*Cupid Jones Gets Married* #1646

## DEANNA TALCOTT

grew up in rural Nebraska, where her love of reading was fostered in a one-room school. It was there she first dreamed of writing the kinds of books that would touch people's hearts. Her dream became a reality when *The Bachelor and the Bassinet,* a Silhouette Romance novel, won the National Readers' Choice award for Best Traditional Romance. Since then, DeAnna has also earned the WISRWA's Readers' Choice Award and the Booksellers' Best Award for the best Traditional Romance. All of her award-winning books have been Silhouette Romance titles!

DeAnna claims a retired husband, three children, two dogs and a matching pair of alley cats make her life in mid-Michigan particularly interesting. When not writing, or talking about writing, she scrounges flea markets to indulge #1 son's quest for vintage toys, relaxes at #2 son's Eastern Michigan football and baseball games, and insists, to her daughter, that two cats simply do not need to multiply!

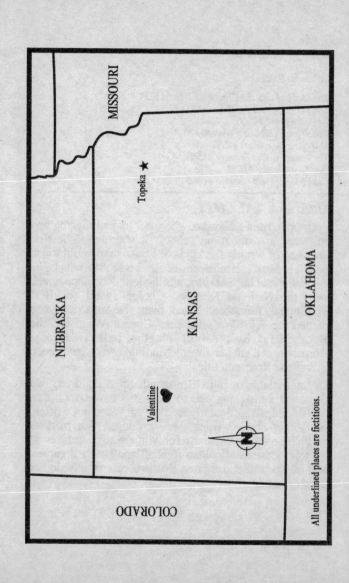

NEBRASKA

MISSOURI

Topeka ★

Valentine

KANSAS

COLORADO

OKLAHOMA

N

All underlined places are fictitious.

# Chapter One

The blonde who idled near the front door of the post office self-consciously patted her hair, then glanced at the clock for the umpteenth time. Cupid, the postmistress of the Valentine, Kansas, branch, peered a little more closely at the patron.

Fine lines bracketed the corners of the woman's blue eyes—*mid-thirties smile lines,* she noted—and the waves in her hair were soft, angelic. Cupid knew—she just *knew*—that the whimsical earrings the woman wore were the most revealing thing about her: 14 carat teddy bears.

The blonde slid Cupid an apprehensive look then walked up to the counter. "I hope I'm not making you uncomfortable, loitering here in the lobby. But I'm meeting my pen pal here, and we both agreed that the post office seemed appropriate."

"Oh, that's okay, it's a public place. People come and go all day."

The blonde nervously worried the single button on her

linen blazer and feigned interest in the snapshot tacked on the bulletin board, while Cupid weighed packages.

"That's Mariah," Cupid explained conversationally. "I took down the FBI's 'most wanted' posters and gave Pop Tomlinson's newest grandchild top billing. Pop loves to brag about his grandchildren, so I thought he'd get a kick out of having her picture up for everyone to admire."

The woman pensively examined the snapshot. "I always wanted to be a mother," she said wistfully. "But well, I *can't*. Have children, I mean."

"Oh. I'm sorry. I—"

"Oh, please. No. Don't apologize. Look," she said, extending her hand, "my name's Moira." Cupid noted that a mother-of-pearl ring graced Moira's right ring finger; she took that as a sign. "I feel like I should introduce myself, since I seem to be taking up all your time and telling you all my secrets. Of course, I'm sure, in your job, you do get a glimpse into a lot of lives."

A mischievous smile tilted Cupid's mouth. "Yes. You could say that." *But not the way you think.*

They paused for a moment, and when Cupid saw Jake Crowell striding up the front walk to get his mail, inspiration struck. She tried to beat back the inclination, but it was all so logical. Really.

Here was a woman who wanted to be a mother.

Here was Jake, widowed two years and struggling to raise three adorable little girls.

It simply made sense. It did. Besides, she'd gotten a very good feeling about this woman. A very good feeling, indeed.

"What did you say your name was again?" Cupid asked.

"Moira. Moira McPherson."

"And you're from?"

"Chicago. But I'm sort of looking to move here, if—"

"Hi!" Jake's deep voice filled the room. "Got any mail for me?"

Cupid watched the vibration go down Moira's spine. *Done deal,* she thought.

Moira half turned to Jake, tipping her head shyly as she backed out of the way to give him access to the counter. Jake's eyes merely slid in her direction, and he nodded.

Drat it all, they didn't make eye contact.

Cupid frowned and feigned a cursory interest in his mail. "Nothing good. Store stuff." She didn't give it to him immediately, but riffled through the envelopes before putting a rubber band around them. "Jake," she said softly, letting her voice run as thick and smooth as honey, "I don't believe you've met Moira McPherson, have you?"

Jake blinked.

"She's new to town. From Chicago."

He turned, automatically offering his hand.

"Jake Crowell, this is Moira," Cupid intoned carefully. "Moira, meet Jake. He owns the hardware store, but his real job is being a full-time daddy to three of the cutest little girls on these Kansas plains."

"She means I'm widowed," Jake explained, taking Moira's delicate hand in his palm.

"I see. Hello...." Moira looked up. Her crystalline-blue eyes locked with his mocha-dark ones.

The expression on Jake's face turned from smiling to smitten.

*Ping!* Just like *that.*

Smug satisfaction washed through Cupid. Hah! She

was better than Samantha in *Bewitched*. She didn't even have to snap her fingers or wrinkle her nose. One teensy-tiny glance, and love bloomed. You just had to nurture the timing, that's all. Very simple, really.

Cupid sighed, knowing she had faded to dull shades of gray in Jake and Moira's peripheral vision. Ah, well, that's what happened. This love-at-first-sight business did have its drawbacks—it was a thankless job. But, hey, somebody had to do it. Besides, she consoled herself, years from now they'd thank her.

When, after five minutes, the couple was still engrossed in animated conversation, Cupid offered them a benevolent smile and moved on to hand-canceling the stamps.

Yes. Sometimes things happened for a reason. Every time she made a match she told herself that. It had become her mantra. *Sometimes things happen for a reason.*

Then the door opened, and a long shadow fell across the floor and the oblivious couple. Cupid looked up— and caught her breath.

A tall, rangy cowboy wearing dusty boots sauntered into the room, a slight swagger in his gait. Cupid couldn't help herself; she imprinted the sound of his footfalls on her memory—and then his image. Boot-cut jeans, faded at the knees, soft and clean. The dull shine of copper rivets following the mesmerizing motion of his hips. The silver-and-turquoise belt buckle on his flat belly, as defining as the man's own distinctive signature. Above it, a blue plaid cowboy shirt, with pearl snap pockets, hugged his torso.

Cupid's gaze continued to slowly inch up his thick chest, over his muscled shoulders and corded neck, before she looked up—into the most incredibly handsome face she'd ever seen.

Her breath sputtered and died in her lungs. The sweetest ache burrowed behind her breastbone, and her eyelids actually drifted partway closed.

This cowboy's face was made of no-nonsense angles and planes. Square jaw, blunt chin. Broad forehead. Full nose. His cheekbones were sculpted like high plateaus against the valley of his temples. His tobacco-dark hair feathered back, softening the hard edges of his face.

When his smooth, sensuous mouth parted, his eyes glittered, then nearly disappeared behind twin crescents of dark lashes.

*Diamond like,* Cupid thought insanely.

She longed to know the color. Cobalt-blue or gun-metal-gray?

He said something to her, and she stared at him dumbly, conscious only of the timbre of his voice, the cadence of his words, and the way they melodically fit together, like a balm to her soul. He waited, then his eyes flicked to the couple beside him.

Finally, it dawned on Cupid that he expected an answer. She flinched, immediately feeling as if she was two cents short of a first class delivery. "Excuse me?" she quavered. "I had my mind on..." her gaze slipped to his wide shoulders and down his lean, hard belly "...other things," she finished lamely.

His belt buckle seemed to wink at her. Cupid's knees quivered. She didn't like it when inanimate objects appeared to take on a life of their own. It wasn't fair, not where *she* was concerned.

"I'm here to meet a friend," he repeated. "A woman?"

Realization struck like a crushing blow to the heart. "You? You're the pen pal?" Cupid asked, disbelief in her voice.

"Burke Riley," he said, "and I'm here to meet—"

The blond woman, hearing his name, swiveled, reluctantly moving away from Jake as if she were on autopilot. "Burke? Burke Riley?" she questioned.

"Yes." There was a slight hesitation, and Cupid held her breath as Burke's assessing gaze slid over Moira McPherson. "I take it you're Moira?"

"Yes." She paused. "Wait. Excuse me...." Moira turned to Jake, her smile sweet, adoring. "Coffee at the Rusty Nail sounds wonderful. Could you give me a few minutes, and I'll meet you there?"

With his eyes still glued to Moira, Jake nodded and backed toward the door. "Of course. I'll get us the best table. The one in the corner."

The moment he left, Moira snagged Burke's wrist and pulled him away from the wall of brass mailboxes. Feeling like an intruder in her own post office, Cupid watched them surreptitiously.

*Wait a minute. What was going on? She was the one who always pulled the strings.*

"I know what I promised," she heard Moira say, "but it isn't going to work. I've suddenly realized it wasn't meant to be. Maybe, if you'd come fifteen minutes earlier...before I'd met Jake..."

Riley stiffened. "What?"

"It doesn't matter." She waggled a hand toward the door. "The postmistress introduced us...and this is truly a man who seems to be writing on my page. I'm sorry. It's nothing personal. But I'm moving on." Moira took a deep breath, hooked a wrist behind Burke's neck and drew him down to her level. She kissed him on the cheek, causing Cupid an inexplicable twinge of envy. "Goodbye, Burke," Moira said gently before she turned away and slipped outside. "It's over."

Burke pivoted on his boot heel, staring dumbstruck after Moira's softly flared skirt, her fashionable heels. When he whirled back, he pinned Cupid with a surly gaze. "Would you like to tell me what the hell that was all about?" he demanded.

Behind the counter, Cupid squirmed. "I guess...I guess she doesn't want to be your pen pal anymore."

"Excuse me?" His eyes narrowed to slits.

"I think she's written you off as a pen pal," she said quietly.

"Pen pal, hell!" he raged, taking one angry step toward her. "Do you know who that was?"

Before she could stop herself, Cupid took a step back. "No..."

"That was my mail-order bride! And you just gave her away! To someone else!"

Cupid gasped, and a sinking feeling spiraled down her middle, turning her insides to mush. This had never ever happened before. She brought people love, not disappointment. She always picked up on the vibrations—although today they seemed distorted, indistinct. "I didn't give her away," she muttered, looking away. "I introduced her."

"Same difference."

"Well," Cupid fumed, fumbling with a dozen envelopes, and angry at her own mistake, "she wasn't right for you, anyway."

"She wasn't right for me," he repeated, scowling. "And how, exactly, would you know that?"

Cupid pushed the envelopes aside, determined to face the man's fury. "Because she was obviously a hothouse flower. Too fragile for your rough edges."

Burke blinked, and it was then Cupid noticed that his eyes were not gunmetal-gray, but *gunpowder* gray—and they seemed about to explode. "That was one fine look-ing woman who just walked out that door! And I planned a hurry-up courtship and a quickie wedding—all to her specifications. I even compromised myself, agreeing to marry a bride sight-unseen. And then you butted in and introduced her to someone else, and she ends up walking out the door with him, and—"

"Compromised yourself?" Cupid's blood began to boil. "Compromised yourself?" she repeated, her voice rising an octave. "If that's the case, and if that's how you feel about an impending marriage, then I definitely think it worked out for the best."

"And just who do you think you are to interfere in my love life?" he snapped. "Cupid?"

Drawing herself to her full five foot eight inch height, she looked up at him, conscious that he towered a good six inches over her. "Of course I'm Cupid," she said, belligerently thrusting her chin to a don't-mess-with-me angle.

Burke Riley's jaw slid off center. He stared at the woman, who was probably a nut and masquerading in an official postal worker's uniform. Then she tilted the plastic name tag in his direction.

Cupid.

Air whooshed out of his lungs, and he tried to refocus, to reread the name and the fine print beneath.

Cupid Jones, Postmistress, Valentine, Kansas.

"You've got to be kidding me."

A smidgen of relief rolled through Cupid; at least he'd lowered his voice. "I kid you not. My mother was the postmistress in Valentine years ago. She thought it would be a hoot to have a little Cupid to inherit the job. *Cupid*," she emphasized, punching her forefinger against the top button of her shirt. "Yes, Cupid. That would be me."

Burke took her in. All of her.

From the red-gold hair that seemed to spiral and corkscrew about her face to her wide-set eyes, which were clear, sandy-bottomed hazel pools with chips of lapis and lime floating in their depths.

He guessed she must be twenty-five or so, maybe ten years younger than him—yet a light smattering of freckles drifted across her nose and gave her a youthful, pixieish appearance. Against her porcelain complexion, her bow-shaped mouth was a delectable shade of berry red. Her full dimpled cheeks tapered down to a slim jawline and narrow chin, emphasizing her heart-shaped face.

Cupid Jones silently withstood his scrutiny with the strangest confidence, and he had to admire her for that. But there was something else, he told himself. A sense, an aura, something he couldn't define, that clung to her and made her *different.*

Just as quickly, ire surfaced in him, making him dismiss all of Cupid Jones's appealing attributes. He had an agenda, and Cupid Jones, whether she realized it or not, had messed with it, shredding all his carefully laid plans.

He was supposed to get married within the month to Moira McPherson—and he knew from Moira's letters, and the glossy glamour shot she'd enclosed, that she'd do. Even if she hadn't looked exactly like the picture, she didn't strain the eyes. He wouldn't have had to squint to find her fine features, wouldn't have to turn out the lights in his bedroom. From her letters he knew they'd be compatible enough—unless, of course, everything was fabricated.

And somehow that didn't even matter.

The bottom line was he wanted a wife and a traditional life. He simply didn't have the time, or the inclination, to find the perfect match. He was on the down side of thirty-five, and he wasn't getting any younger. There were days he reminded himself of his father, and that scared the hell out of him.

He didn't want to wind up a broken-down, arthritic old man who fumbled with diapers for late-in-life babies. He didn't want to grow into an ornery old cuss, too set in his ways to appreciate his wife, or, when he was wrong, spit out an occasional "I'm sorry, I made a mistake" to his kids.

This arranged marriage thing wasn't a lonely hearts deal, it was a practical solution for a western plains rancher who lived fifty miles from nowhere. Fifty miles from the place most folks jokingly referred to as the romance capital of the world. He'd hoped it would bring him a little luck, to meet his potential bride there, at the post office where once a year they canceled valentines with a stamp that said Love Blooms in Valentine, Kansas.

Well, it hadn't done him a bit of good, had it?

He planted his feet and squared his shoulders, purposely allowing a bit of intimidation into his stance. "Well, Miss Cupid," he drawled, "you gave away my bride, and I don't appreciate that. So you can just find me another. And you've got three weeks to do it."

*Chapter Two*

Cupid sputtered. "It doesn't work like that!" she protested.

"Like what?"

"I can't just find you a bride and make you a match because you ask. The conditions have to be... I mean—" She broke off, knowing she'd already said too much. She tried to bluff her way through and started babbling instead. "I mean...well, gracious, look at me. If I had a knack for this kind of thing, I'd find myself a husband. If I had those powers, I mean. Why, I've been the bridesmaid in thirteen weddings, and I'm still not married. Not even once. Always the bridesmaid, never the bride."

His gaze narrowed. "Unlucky number," he said, his eyes boring into her.

"Excuse me?"

"Thirteen. Unlucky number."

Cupid shrugged, immensely relieved he hadn't picked up on the rest of it. She didn't intend to tell him she had introduced every one of those couples—and there were countless couples she'd introduced who *hadn't* included her in their wedding. "I know," she agreed. "But coming up is fourteen. Now that's my lucky number. I figure the next one's definitely—"

"Pardon?" he interrupted. "Did you say...fourteen? As in February 14?"

Her mother claimed that on the day of her birth, the sun, the moon, and the stars were aligned for a phenomenon. That, coupled with a little help from her genes, had shaped and directed her powers. Even so, to mere mortals, Cupid dismissed her powers as a 'gift.' No one actually knew she made matches by a mere introduction.

Jake, this is Moira.

Moira, meet Jake.

It was her destiny to make matches, to see to it that people fell in love and lived happily ever after. The job at the post office just paid the bills.

"I suppose Moira mentioned she wanted to get married on February 14," Burke remarked.

The significance struck a raw nerve. "On my birthday?" Cupid asked without thinking.

He paused, staring at her intently. "February 14— Valentine's Day?—is your birthday?"

"Yes—well, no—I mean, Moira didn't tell me about that. If I'd known..." Cupid sucked in a deep, cleansing breath, and struggled to make sense of this new revelation. It had implications. Definite implications.

"You'd have done what?"

"Why, I'd have warned her against it," Cupid declared, wondering if she was in over her head with this man, and all the suggestive baggage he'd unwittingly brought with him. "Look at me. It was just my dumb luck to be born on Valentine's Day. It's an overblown holiday, and with a name like Cupid, I'm the target of every joke. If I was smart, I'd move as far away from Valentine as I could get, change my name to Aphrodite and—''

"Aphrodite?" He inclined his head, as if he wasn't sure he'd heard her correctly.

She nodded.

"Aphrodite," he repeated. "Now there's a nice, common, middle-of-the-road name. Yeah. Sure. I can see why you'd want to hide behind that."

Cupid blanched. How did this man keep doing this to her, to get her to reveal all her secrets? Around him, the more she talked, the more she talked. "Aphrodite's my middle name," she grudgingly admitted. "My mother? She was not one to leave a stone unturned."

"Apparently not," he agreed blandly. "And, out of curiosity, your mother would be...?"

"Venus," Cupid replied.

He arched a brow in disbelief, his mouth curling.

Cupid wanted to crawl into the cubbyhole under the counter. He'd done it again! She straightened and busied herself with the bundle of envelopes she'd finished hand-canceling. "That's Mrs. Jones to you," she clarified brusquely. "My mother is a sedate, proper, gray-haired grandmother—and she doesn't let just anyone go around calling her by her first name."

"And I suppose," he said, his voice edged with sarcasm, "it was your mother, Mrs. Jones, who was the inspiration for that popular Frankie Avalon tune. The one that was such a hit?"

Inside, Cupid winced and tamped down her discomfort. Few people knew the truth behind *that* story. Most people were content to believe the song was about a young man's yearnings. "Of course, my mother would love to take credit," Cupid said loftily. "Who wouldn't? But the truth is, she's had a very simple life right here in Valentine. Now, she did introduce an old maid aunt over in Stoverville to her fourth cousin—once removed, and thrice divorced—on her father's side. But that's the only love connection she ever brags about."

*And how many were there her mother didn't brag about?*

*It would boggle the mind.*

Cupid smiled sweetly, innocently, back at him and tried not to think of her mother's compulsion for making matches. Three years ago, she'd claimed she was going to retire, but she was still at it—every time inspiration and the right inclination struck.

Burke rocked back on his heels, considering. "Cupid. Cupid Aphrodite..." He tried the name experimentally, rolling it around on his tongue. "Cupid, daughter of Venus."

"Venus Pandora Jones," Cupid automatically supplied.

Both his dark brows rose. "Pandora?"

What was happening to her? The man barely looked at her, and she ended up spilling family secrets without batting so much as an eyelash! There were only a handful of people who knew her mother's given name. And here Cupid had uttered it just as brazenly to a total stranger as if he was a long-time, and trusted friend.

"Grandma knew Mom was going to be a handful," she improvised. "Called her a real Pandora's box of trouble." Burke Riley stared at her in an uncanny, perceptive way. Cupid grew uncomfortably hot. "It's a...a family joke." She endured another second of silence. "She'd kill me if she knew I'd told you her whole name."

"Oh." He lifted both hands, shrugging. "I won't tell." Then he muttered under his breath, "Nobody'd believe me anyway." He shook his head and raised his voice. "Out of curiosity, your father's name would be...? Because if you say Zeus or Hercules or—"

"Bob," she supplied. "Bob Jones. Plain, simple and very common." *Very common.* No special powers—save for his extraordinary patience with all the women in his family. Thank the stars her sister, Lysandra, had found a job in a bridal boutique in Loveknot, Texas.

Suddenly, without warning, Burke leaned closer and planted both elbows on the counter. He put his face just magnetizing inches from hers. "Even so, with names like that," he stated, his voice running smooth as honey, "you must feel an obligation to live up to the love, romance and marriage thing."

He was so close, she could smell the essence of him. All male. With human frailties. A crazy mixture of soap and sweat, leather and liniment.

Cupid's blood started thrumming, and a rushing sound echoed in her ears, vibrating clear through to her soul and making her world tilt and spin in crazy, rose-colored shades.

Focus was impossible; all she could see were Burke's disturbing gray eyes.

"I'd like one wedding, one bride," he ordered. "I don't care what it costs or how you do it. You arrange everything. Including the bride."

Cupid went weak and her mouth sagged. "It isn't that easy. I can't just go *presto-chango*—" she snapped her fingers "—and come up with a bride!"

"Hey. You gave mine away."

"I didn't—"

"A bride, Cupid. The sooner, the better."

"Why?" she said in frustration. "Why are you so determined to get married? Especially to someone you don't even know! Mail-order brides are a thing of the past. You should—"

"I want to settle down," he interrupted, "with female companionship. I've spent the last twenty years of my life with a contrary herd of shorthorns, or a rowdy bunkhouse of cowboys. I'm ready to move on to quieter things."

"Yes, and getting you a bride isn't like culling an available heifer out of the herd," she snapped. "It isn't like coming up with an Annie Oakley and asking her to put down her six-shooter and start baking cookies."

One tension-filled second slipped away. "It's time," he said firmly. "I have a nice life, and I want to share it."

"But listen, you're a…" She groped for the right word. *Hunk, hottie, hardbody* all surfaced in her mind; none of them were right. She cleared her throat noisily. "You're an *attractive* man," she said finally, carefully. "You wouldn't have any trouble meeting women. Heck, the women would probably find you if you gave them half a chance."

"I don't have the time and I don't have the inclination," he said, pushing himself away from the counter. "I live on a ranch fifty miles from Valentine, and I don't relish the idea of parading a bunch of bride wannabe's over the threshold and introducing them to my way of life. I don't want to fiddle around with the getting-to-know-you phase, and I don't want to have someone measure me with a compatibility quotient, or hit me up with a set of demands. It shouldn't be this complicated. I just want a wife I can ride off into the sunset with."

"You're dreaming. It doesn't work like that."

"How about you?" he asked, undaunted. "You're not married."

The offhand proposal went zinging like a shot to her heart. For a split second, her breath actually left her. Then she bristled. "Don't be ridiculous! That's the most outrageous, incredible suggestion I've ever—"

He shrugged apologetically. "You might be a little outspoken, and a little prickly, but I figure I could make it work. You'd probably simmer right down after we got through the intimate details."

The pointblank suggestion should have spurred her feminine side to another round of indignation. Instead, the fleeting thought of intimacy with Burke Riley whirled through her head like a merry-go-round of wild colors and dizzying expectations. Cupid trembled, then suddenly grew skittish. "Well, I couldn't," she said flatly, dismissing the idea, "and I wouldn't." She hesitated. "Most women, including me, have this warped idea that they will only marry for love. I know it's a revolutionary concept, especially for cowboys with caveman attitudes."

He grimaced, his eyes going flat, hard. "I've heard," he said, "that in arranged marriages, people fall in love after the wedding. I reckon it's about like putting the cart before the horse."

"You, as a cowboy, would make that comparison."

"Whatever it takes to get there, honey."

"You don't get it. Women don't even need men anymore. They are independent, self-assured, resourceful. So getting you a wife...well, it isn't as easy as..." She stared into the smoky depths of his flinty gaze and promptly forgot her argument.

"Yes?"

"I—I'm thinking...."

"About what?"

"About everything, if you must know."

That was the problem. She saw everything about Burke too clearly. His honesty. His forthright nature. His determination to marry.

Her imagination painted vivid pictures, the most vivid she'd ever experienced. Burke Riley astride a roan mare and checking a fenceline. Burke Riley shirtless, a pitchfork in one hand, a beat-up straw hat tipped to the back of his head.

Burke Riley alone at his kitchen table, with no one to share the second cup of coffee…or to share the gathering dusk, and the endless highway of stars above his ranch at midnight.

She could see it, the infinite stretch of a solitary existence, from the day of his birth until the hour he'd driven into Valentine to pick up Moira, his mail-order bride. He'd told Cupid he wanted a wife. He'd said he had a nice life, and he wanted to share it.

In her avocation, she'd certainly heard a lot of poor reasons for wanting a mate. She'd made matches because it "felt" right, because she detected a need for a fuller, richer life, for love. Perhaps this man, Burke Riley, was a valid candidate for a match.

Still, she didn't grant requests randomly…

The imperceptible current swirling about him was a drawback. It wrought havoc on her intuition and affected her judgment. She should have known that he and Moira…

Cupid made a hasty decision. It would be best to get rid of him, to make the match and dismiss the chaos he'd created in her senses. It wasn't worth compromising her powers because he'd ignited a little static in her energy field.

"Okay," she said suddenly, "I know almost everyone in and around Valentine. I could probably introduce you to someone who would make a satisfactory bride. But no guarantees, you understand. I'll do my best, and beyond that it's up to you."

"Just like that?"

"Just like—" Cupid raised her hand and snapped her fingers "—that."

Burke's smile broadened. "Then it's a date, honey. As long as I'm in town, we'll have dinner and seal the deal."

## Chapter Three

Cupid didn't have a clue as to why she agreed to have dinner with Burke Riley. She walked ahead of him, into the Swingin' Door Steakhouse, and was extraordinarily piqued to see Flora Williams draped against the bar. Flora, recently divorced, was looking. And she was looking straight at Burke.

When Cupid glanced over her shoulder and saw Burke return Flora's come-hither smile, she beat back an inexplicable surge of irritation.

Burke leaned provocatively close to Cupid's ear, raising the fine hairs on her nape. "Introduce me to that one," he whispered.

Cupid abruptly turned away, her elbow raking his solar plexus, as she sought an out-of-the-way table on the *other* side of the bar, away from Flora. "Not your type, Burke," she warned briskly. "That one is definitely not your ride-off-into-the-sunset kind of girl."

Burke pulled out her chair, then nudged out his own

and sat, his face pinched with annoyance. "I thought you were going to introduce me around."

"I am. But we need to talk a little first. Let me get a handle on you, what you're about and what you want."

"I want a wife," he said succinctly.

"I know that. You've made it perfectly clear. But don't you want one that lasts? Flora's not the sticking type."

"Flora? Her name's Flora?" Burke sidled another glance over to the bar, and Flora's smile spread, oozing across her features like the nectar from a deadly Venus's fly trap.

"Yes," Cupid said, reclaiming his attention, "and unlike the flora and fauna indigenous to this area, that particular 'Flora' wilts very quickly. She doesn't transplant well. Certainly not to the conditions you're proposing." Cupid whipped the white paper napkin off the table, then shook it out and made a show of spreading it on her lap and smoothing out the creases.

An edge of disappointment marked Burke's features, and Cupid took note, mentally recording the data.

Naive. Burke Riley was naive. Particularly with women who had been around the block—and Flora had a notorious reputation for waltzing, two-stepping and sidestepping through Valentine's pristine fields of testosterone. Burke Riley was a mere babe in the woods compared to Flora.

Sympathy washed through Cupid. She had to protect him. "Tell me about your ranch," she said, changing the subject.

Burke pulled two menus from the metal clip and handed her one. "Not much to tell. My dad put me on a horse at six months, and I pretty much grew up with four legs and a quarter horse gait beneath me."

"I see. He was a real cowboy, then."

"No, he was a hard-drinkin' son-of-a-bitch who made his living as a horse trader. There's a difference." Burke paused and, unaware of Cupid's stricken reaction, flipped a page of the plastic-coated menu. "Went by the name of Punch—and he was the kind of guy who figured if I saw the world from the back of a quarter horse, he'd done his job."

His bald explanation surprised Cupid, making her intentionally neutralize her response. "So. You've spent your whole life around horses."

Burke smiled blandly and closed the menu. "You could say that. But you introduce me to some woman, you remember I'm a *rancher,* not a cowboy."

She stared at him. *What had she gotten herself into?*

"My father," he explained, "didn't cut anyone any slack. Not his wife. Not his kid. The only thing he knew how to gentle was a high plains mustang. Well, I don't want Punch Riley's reputation tainting mine. His marriage may have crumbled, but I refuse to let that happen to me, no matter what."

Cupid silently shuddered, but filed the information in her data banks. "So you've chosen to concentrate on ranching, not horses or—"

"I raise some of the finest quarter horses in the country—thanks to the old man's influence. He set me up, and my mother kicked in for four years at Texas A & M, so I have a degree to handle the business side of ranching."

"Oh, I see…. It sounds like you were raised by your mother, then."

"No." He took the menu Cupid had closed and slid it with his back into the metal clip fastened to the wall. "She left when I was six. My father said she was free to go, but I was staying put. Said no kid of Punch Riley's was going to end up a citified sissy, wearing short pants and playing in a rock band."

"My. I guess your father was quite a character."

Burke snorted. "Always had a burr under his saddle, no question there."

Doubts about what she was doing riddled Cupid, and she was compelled to voice her concerns. "Burke? Are you sure you want to do this? Get married, I mean. From what you're saying, I think you might have a slightly skewed view of what a marriage and a family might involve. I mean, I get the impression you didn't grow up watching *The Brady Bunch* or *The Partridge Family*."

"I only watched reruns. *Ponderosa, Rawhide* and *The Wild, Wild West*."

In spite of herself, Cupid smiled. "My point is—"

Burke reached across the table, his palm settling across her forearm, exerting light pressure. A ticklish sensation skittered up her arm, making Cupid uneasy— aware and wary at the same time. "I know what your point is," he said softly, his voice low and deadly serious. "You don't have to explain it. I guarantee you I'm not the reflection of my father. And I'm certainly not like my mother. I don't run when things get tough, and I'm hard, but I don't browbeat people to get what I want. Nothing scares me, Cupid. And nothing is too hard for me to handle. Nothing. Certainly not a woman."

Sensuous implications peppered his declaration.

Within her chest, Cupid's breath grew light and fluttery. Inertia gripped her. As long as his hand held her fast, she was unable to move, to rationally respond. There were dozens of arguments, but she couldn't think of any. Not right now. Not while his face loomed across the table, carved with shadows by the tiny flickering votive candle on the table.

Certainly she witnessed strength within Burke Riley, but she also perceived a weakness—one she couldn't identify—and it baffled her. Burke was an enigma, the hard silent type every woman wanted to tame. Cupid felt an inexplicable craving to know more about this curious man.

His fingers gently relaxed, peeling one by one from the fine bones above her wrist.

"Now…" he said quietly, redirecting her attention, "a young woman just came in, with her parents, I think. The brunette over there. What about her?"

"She's too—" Cupid blinked, aware that a denial was already on her lips. She hadn't even looked at the woman, for heaven's sake! "Young," she revised lamely, trying to cover her gaffe.

"Young? She looks like an old maid spinster."

Cupid took in the rail-thin woman. "Oh. Her. That's Clare Vollner," she whispered, surprised that Burke would even consider her, with her plain looks and jerky, birdlike movements. "She's led a sheltered life. A late-in-life baby who still lives at home and cares for her parents. So when I said 'young,' I meant in…worldly experience."

"Uh-huh."

"See how devoted she is to her parents? A good quality, yes. But I can tell you right off the bat that that would be a stumbling block. I mean, *look*.…"

Clare fussily straightened her elderly father's lapel, then offered her mother a packet of medication and a glass of water to take it with.

"Let me get this right," he said slowly. "According

to you, I've chosen one that's too worldly, and one not worldly enough.''

"In my opinion, you've gone from one extreme to the other," Cupid commented idly, lifting a shoulder. "Give it time. Don't be so impatient."

Cupid's advice lingered in the back of Burke's mind as they gave their orders to the waitress. Later, as they ate, his attention strayed to the dining patrons, then drifted back to Cupid. She was bright, witty and charming...and she seemed delighted to shift the focus away from his prospective bride and entertain him with post office stories.

His gaze dropped to her lips. So mesmerizing to watch the way the corners lifted as she laughed, to see the way her mouth puckered before she delivered the punch line, or raised, just slightly, to expose the pearly edge of a tooth.

He smiled to himself, thinking that "playing post office" with Cupid would put a whole new twist on the game.

"They insisted I take the week off before Valentine's Day this year," she confided, dabbing at her mouth with a napkin. "Last year, they said I caused a near riot. Of course, it wasn't me, exactly, but my name. And the fact I was there. Everyone wants their valentines hand-canceled by Cupid. For good luck or something."

Burke chuckled. Yet her comment reminded him of his own intention to give himself every advantage by meeting Moira at the Valentine post office. It had *seemed* like a good idea at the time, especially for a mail-order bride.

"At one point," she added, "I had people standing in line right out to the sidewalk, in snow two feet deep."

He shook his head, imagining.

"One guy wanted me to seal his envelope with a kiss, and another brought a special tube of lipstick and asked me to imprint all of his envelopes with the touch of my lips."

Burke raised one eyebrow, then the other.

The tip of Cupid's tongue flicked over her upper lip, moistening it. "I didn't do it," she said. "I couldn't. It would have taken too long—he must have had forty Valentines. And people at the back of the line were getting a little testy by that time."

"They think you have special powers," Burke said finally.

"They *want* to believe that," she clarified. She smiled mysteriously. "It's amazing what the power of suggestion will do."

"So that's what you're going to do for me. Suggest some potential wives, make a few introductions..."

Cupid's smile tightened. "Exactly. And then you're on your own. Whatever happens happens."

Burke flipped a credit card onto the table, barely scanning the bill before the waitress whisked it away. "Who will you choose for me, Cupid?" he asked.

"Who do you want?"

"Someone faithful and hardworking. Sturdy. Smart, with common sense. Someone who isn't afraid to get dirty—"

She held her hand up, stopping him. "Wait a minute. Sure you aren't looking for a Girl Scout? Or...maybe a lap dog?"

He chuckled appreciatively. "Someone with a sense of humor," he finished. "Someone like you."

The waitress plopped the guest check on the table, and

Burke picked it up, signing with a flourish and missing Cupid's reaction.

"Your qualifications remind me of someone," she said vaguely. "I just can't remember who." She shrugged. "Probably already taken. The good ones usually are."

"Great," he said drolly. "That gives me a lot of hope."

She laughed. "Don't get discouraged before we even start," she warned. "I'm not going to have trouble finding you a wife—but I want to make sure everything's in order so that we can find you the perfect woman. How do you argue with that?" She slid out of the booth, and looked over her shoulder at Burke.

For a split second he witnessed a twinkle in her eye, and it stopped him cold. He'd never seen anything like it before. One crystal blue spark—as pure as the heat from heaven, as promising as the descent into hell.

A shudder vibrated through his chest, and he felt transported outside his physical body. Inside, he was warm and floating. His thoughts were not his own. A craving, one he'd never experienced, was unleashed, and it rushed through his veins. He was momentarily convinced his inclinations were being guided by another, greater power.

Just as quickly, he made a conscious effort to struggle against the feelings, and fought his way back to reality. He planted his boots firmly on the hardwood floor, stiffening his spine. With his hands curled into fists, he made his mind go blank.

*To hell with this. He didn't dally in La-la-land.*

The world came back into focus, Cupid's head bobbing ahead of him like a beacon.

He blinked, telling himself there had to be some explanation for the brief mental departure. A phenomenon. The way the bar lighting struck Cupid's eyes, the way the overhead disco ball sent scintillating sparks through the dimly lit eating area.

*The sparkle of a vibrant woman.*

By the time they were outside, Burke had already dismissed the unsettling moment. He dealt in the here and now. "So we've got a deal then, and you're serious about finding me a wife."

"Absolutely."

"You're not just putting me on?"

"I'll take full credit for giving your mail-order bride away," she declared. "And I'll find you someone else."

He stared down into her face. He heard the teasing note in her voice, and it elicited the strangest tremor in his middle. "My old man had a saying," he said, gauging her reaction as his hand slipped beneath her elbow. "He said with a man you seal a deal with a handshake…with a woman, you seal it with a kiss." He was gratified to see her eyes widen, exposing clear, innocent depths. Her mouth parted slightly, the bow shape collapsing into a surprised, vulnerable O.

He couldn't resist. Not if his life had depended on it.

"Just for luck," he wheedled, bending closer. "For you. And me. And this upcoming marriage."

When she didn't offer a whit of resistance, he claimed her. She was soft in all the right places, her curves pressed against his chest, her belly molding against his belt buckle, the thrust of his hips. Their legs tangled as they swayed on the slab of cement.

His heart started hammering, sparks ignited and pistons started firing, like an engine roaring to life. An unfamiliar rhythm took over, pumping a new madness within him.

*Woman,* his subconscious affirmed, *and you need her.*

But this was a mistake…he was kissing Cupid, the *wrong* woman!

Burke reluctantly, but deftly pulled away from her pliant lips. Cupid's eyes were still closed, but her lids fluttered. Her defenseless demeanor preyed on him, and he felt inordinately guilty for taking advantage of her. He'd intended the gesture as something careless and casual; his reaction, was anything but.

He slowly, carefully, propped her back on her feet.

"Cupid?"

"Yes…?"

Her breath was light, quivery, and she put a hand on his chest.

"Cupid, hey!" a female voice interrupted, as someone stepped up beside them.

Cupid's head swiveled, and she obviously grappled to make the connection. "Jane?" A second slipped away. "Oh. Jane. Hi! How are you?"

"Great. Just meeting Greg and Marcy for dinner. It's a Tuesday night thing." The tall, definitely single, woman looked expectantly at Burke.

In spite of what had just happened between himself and Cupid, Burke refused to let even one opportunity slip through his fingers. He smiled broadly, then looked down at Cupid. "Aren't you going to introduce me to your friend?" he prompted.

Cupid flinched as if he'd pinched her. "No. I'm not."

He pulled back, unable to wipe the surprise from his features. "What?"

"I can't."

"You *can't?*"

Cupid shifted uncomfortably. "It's just that, um…" she gnawed on her lower lip "…Jane's late. She always runs late. Greg and Marcy are probably waiting for her right now.''

Jane, unaffected, tossed her head and laughed. ''You know me like a book, Cupid. It's my fatal flaw, I admit it. I always run fifteen minutes behind the rest of the world.'' Patting her friend on the arm, the woman looked Burke straight in the eye and said, ''Maybe next time, cowboy. When you don't have your hands full with Cupid.''

# Chapter Four

While Burke drove her home, Cupid stole surreptitious glances at him. Her mouth still tingled, and occasionally she gnawed on her lower lip, to see if she could still taste the beer he'd had with his steak.

Now *that* had been a kiss. A mind-boggling, weak-to-the-tips-of-your-toes kind of kiss. She'd literally melted. Her limbs had felt as heavy as honey, her heart started yammering in her chest and a kaleidoscope of fireworks went off behind her eyelids.

Frankly, it had been one humdinger of a kiss.

And it had rattled her, almost upending her data banks.

She had never been kissed like that in her entire life. And then to be kissed on the front stoop of the steak house, beneath the flashing neon lights, and with one of her prospective clients...why, it was almost indecent.

She glanced at Burke once more from beneath lowered lashes.

He was an incredible male specimen, and a far cry

from the gangly, geeky teens she'd dated in high school. Their kisses had been amateurish at best. Burke's had been powerful, masterful.

She briefly considered the two-year relationship she'd had after high school. It had been friendly, cordial and very platonic. Roger was an outgoing, gregarious man, but his overtures in the romance department could at best be described as fluttery, even feeble. He'd had all the qualifications for a good husband and a good father, yet his kisses were affectionate, nothing more. He just didn't have *it*—that chemistry thing—and Cupid knew settling for less would be a compromise, one she could ill afford to make.

"Music?" Burke asked, interrupting Cupid's wayward thoughts.

"Yes. That would be nice." She watched the confident, controlled way he handled the sedan. With one hand on the wheel, he fiddled with the radio, adjusting the volume of the back speaker.

"Okay?" he asked, after choosing a mellow station, with familiar, recognizable tunes.

"Perfect. Yes."

He listened to a few bars of the music, then snorted, never taking his eyes from the road. "You know, I had this fantasy that you would find me a wife tonight."

"Really? You thought I'd come up with a wife for you just like that?"

"Mmm. I know it sounds crazy, but I got this feeling. That maybe you knew someone, or…" He trailed off, lifting a shoulder. "Hey, I don't know."

Cupid hesitated, wondering vaguely if he doubted her abilities. "Tell me. Why are you in such a hurry to get married, anyway? Most men want to avoid the altar."

"Take a look. I'm not getting any younger. I hit thirty-five six months ago."

Since he offered the invitation, Cupid blatantly trailed a long, assessing look over him. Physically, Burke was in the prime of his life. He was a hardbody, lean through the belly and wide through the shoulders. Most women would fall all over themselves, they'd be so attracted to him. She was. "So you're a thirty-something bachelor," she said. "There's a lot of them around these days."

"Oh, you know that? I suppose you also know a lot of them?"

The tone of Burke's voice made Cupid squirm uncomfortably. Was he flirting with her? The possibility both intrigued and surprised her. "Me? No. But I know a lot of people," she said. "I have this penchant for..." She stopped herself from telling him too much. "Befriending people," she revised. "Like Moira. When she came into the post office this afternoon."

His mouth firmed and a slight shadow creased his brow. "Ah, yes. Moira."

"You'd never actually met her before?"

Burke fixed his gaze on the narrow strip of blacktop. "Nope."

"And she started out as a pen pal and wound up a mail-order bride?"

"Sort of," he said evasively.

"No. Don't tell me." Cupid clutched her chest, unable to fathom the lengths to which mortals went to find love and romance. "You didn't meet her through an ad in a lonely hearts magazine, did you?"

"What difference would it make if I did?" Burke huffed. "The woman writes a real nice letter. You can tell a lot about a person that way."

"Enough to marry her?"

"That was the general idea."

Cupid rolled her eyes and looked out the window.

"Well, it isn't that much different than going to a dating service, or meeting someone through a chat room, or going to a bar."

Cupid bit her tongue. Dating services, modern technology and bar-hopping certainly cut into her business. "I guess. It just doesn't make sense that you, of all people, would have to resort to a...a—"

"What's that supposed to mean?" he interrupted. "Me, of all people?"

"Well, think about it. You're..." she took a deep, calming breath "...*reasonably* attractive," she said. Liar. The man could pose for a *GQ* cover.

"Reasonably," he repeated.

Cupid swallowed. "I'm trying to be fair."

"Fine. Go on."

"You, um, appear focused, and hardworking. Honest. Nice..." *Sexy.* Cupid shook herself, wondering where that had come from. She needed distance. Professional distance. "I'd think you'd want to get to know someone, in person. To see if you're compatible. To see if you enjoy being with them."

"I got to know Moira through letters. It was good enough for me."

"Did you..." Cupid hesitated for a split second "...fall in love with her?"

"Love? What's love got to do with it?" Burke looked genuinely surprised. "Moira was a nice person. I figured things like that—that love and mushy stuff—would work out eventually."

Cupid eyes widened, but she tried to neutralize her response. "But I think love's a nice beginning, particularly if you intend to spend the rest of your life with someone. If you're going to marry them. You know,'' she prompted, ''you kiss them and wind up feeling a little…'' she cleared her throat, the memory of his kiss too fresh, too clear in her mind ''…giddy and light-headed and—''

His head swiveled, and he looked at her directly. ''Wait a minute. Are we talking sex? Or love?''

Cupid felt deflated, as if he'd popped her balloon with a pin. ''Typical. That is such a male response,'' she muttered. ''I can't believe I'm wasting my time with you.''

Burke, unaffected, lifted one shoulder in a shrug.

''No, I'm talking about experiencing this…this bond,'' Cupid said, ''this connection between two people. Where you care about someone. Where you worry about them.''

''Oh, that. I figured that would develop in time. I didn't walk into that post office expecting love at first sight, anyhow.''

''Hold it.'' Cupid raised her voice and her hand. ''You don't believe in love at first sight?''

''No. I don't.''

''Well, it can happen,'' Cupid declared testily, ''and it does. I've witnessed it. I've seen people literally swept off their feet. One glance. One look, and they're gone. Gone!'' She snapped her fingers. ''Just like that.''

Burke lifted his foot from the accelerator and let the car slow. His smile was sardonic, and one eyebrow inched higher than the other. ''Head over heels in love, huh?''

Cupid nodded emphatically.

''And you've seen it happen?''

''On more than one occasion.''

He chuckled. ''Well, honey,'' he drawled, ''it ain't gonna happen to me.''

Indignation welled in Cupid. Apparently he hadn't been affected by that kiss they'd shared, not one little bit. "That's because you refuse to open yourself to the possibilities."

"Oh? Really?"

"Really. If you'd just let things happen...instead of hunting down a wife like you're on a scavenger hunt or something—"

"A scavenger hunt," he repeated. "You know, I've never been on a scavenger hunt."

"Well, I get the impression you're on one now. What if you'd discovered you didn't even *like* Moira? Would you have gone through with it anyway?"

He considered, stepping on the accelerator after they turned a corner. "Look. I walked into that post office, figuring that this thing wasn't much different than a business proposal. She puts her name on one dotted line, I put my name on the other."

"Oh, my stars—"

"But I'm not going to make my life miserable, if that's what you mean. The bottom line is that I really don't believe in love, and romance, and that happily-ever-after stuff. It's a nice idea, but real life just doesn't happen that way."

That was not the statement Cupid wanted to hear. She wanted Burke to echo her sentiments about love and romance and marriage. She wanted something definitive, something with substance.

Instead, he'd told her about lonely hearts magazines, and putting his name on the dotted line like it was a business deal! He didn't believe in love at first sight, and he made it perfectly clear he didn't believe in love and romance. Apparently he thought happy endings only happened in the movies.

Well, he was wrong, wrong, wrong!

Although she was still a novice, Cupid knew love wasn't rational, or sensible. It was wacky and wonderful and unpredictable. It wasn't something you did with your head, but with your heart.

The best thing she could do for Burke was prove it to him.

The prospect ahead of her was nothing less than daunting.

Maybe she'd bit off too much this time, and overestimated her powers. Burke Riley had definitely tossed a little snow on her screen, and everything was turning out fuzzy. That dratted kiss—though unexpected—bordered on personal involvement. A definite no-no.

According to the *St. Valentine's Handbook for Apprenticeship, Numinous Exploration and Matchmaking,* personal involvement could compromise her gift. It probably already had. Her thinking was skewed. She could feel it.

She should enlist the aid of her mother—her mother always knew what to do in matters of the heart. It would be the prudent thing to do: let Mom smite Burke with a wife.

But her mom was leaving tomorrow for the twenty-fifth annual Heart and Soul Convention in San Francisco. Her father, recently retired from the phone company, intended to accompany her, claiming this was their second honeymoon, and he didn't mind sharing it with Matchmakers of the First Order.

No. Cupid would do this by herself. No matter what the consequences. If she got into real trouble she'd call her sister, Lysandra.

In the meantime, she intended to prove Burke Riley

wrong. She'd make him fall in love, whether he wanted to or not.

"Burke," she said finally, "I'm really not sure you're marriage material. But I'll do my best to pawn you off on someone. I swear I will."

# Chapter Five

Burke couldn't help thinking about Cupid. It was as if his thoughts just drifted over and settled on her. The woman was amazing. She was funny and charming and kind. She had a sort of timeless beauty and an instinct, a knowledge or understanding, that surpassed her twenty-five years.

It was the goofiest thing. He came home and kept thinking about *her*. Cupid. He wondered how she'd like his home, his life. He wondered if she'd ever been on a working ranch before. He wondered if she rode. He wondered if he could teach her to ride.

He had the nicest little strawberry roan mare....

He thought about how Cupid would look astride that horse. He kept imagining a lazy day with the two of them on horses, laughing—an entire day, instead of the brief hours they'd spent at the Swingin' Door Steakhouse.

He imagined helping her into the saddle. He imagined helping her down. He imagined his hands on her waist.

He imagined kissing her again. Maybe with her back pressed against the heaving side of that little roan, and the smells of leather and horses and spring all around them.

Geez, thoughts like that just about got his shorts in a hitch.

And that made him think about the ridiculous comment Cupid had made about love and sex. Or…had it been his ridiculous comment?

He guessed he'd never really thought about the differences before. He just assumed people got married and were together. That was it. A couple. A pair. An arrangement, for life.

Two months ago, he'd figured Moira was the easy way out. Just marry her and be done with it. He wouldn't have to put out much effort in the getting-to-know-you phase, and there wouldn't be much time to second-guess each other, either.

Yet, strangely enough, he'd dismissed all thoughts of Moira seconds after she'd waltzed out the post office door, traipsing after that hardware guy.

It had been for the best, no doubt about it. One whiff of that rosewater she'd bathed in was enough to convince him she was too prissy and not cut out to be a rancher's wife. Why, his stock would catch the scent of that and probably bolt for higher ground.

It was ten o'clock on a Friday night…three days since he'd last seen or spoken to Cupid. It seemed like an eternity, especially when he had her on his mind all the time. He fixed his gaze on the television set and tried to concentrate on the weather report; it was the only reason he stayed up this late.

Unseasonably warm highs for January. High sixties, possibly seventies. Sunshine.

Burke took the forecast as a sign. No, better yet, as an invitation.

Tomorrow was Saturday. Cupid worked a half day; she'd told him that. The afternoon would be balmy and beautiful and perfect for riding.

Heedless of the hour, he picked up the phone and called her. By the third ring, a glimmer of guilt niggled him. It was late. Maybe he was making a mistake in calling her.

"Hello?"

Her voice was like a breath of fresh air. "Cupid?"

"Yes, and this would be...Burke?" She sounded pleased. He wondered vaguely if that was because he'd called or because she'd guessed who he was. "My. You sound exactly the same on the phone."

"I do?"

"You've got an, um, distinctive voice."

His chest swelled a little, to think that she'd noticed or even remembered. "Figured I ought to call and check in, to see how the bride-hunt is coming."

"Bride-hunt?" She laughed. "Hah. Yes, you would call it that. And I ought to call it a witch-hunt. There's absolutely no one out there for you, Burke. No one," she teased.

He chuckled. Damn, the woman was quick-witted! Why, she made him feel more alive than he had in years. "Don't tell me you've given up already."

"Me? Absolutely not. But I've decided to go about this systematically."

"You have?"

"Certainly. And right now I'm eliminating people that aren't right for you."

He considered. "Anyone left?" he asked mildly.

Over the phone, he could actually feel her smile. "I'm

not telling. But it's not looking good.'' Again he heard that teasing lilt.

"Supposed to be a nice day tomorrow,'' he ventured. "Figured maybe I could drive into Valentine tomorrow afternoon and we could talk it out. Go for a ride or something.''

Burke heard a click, as if Cupid had fumbled with the phone. "Um, yes. I can do that.''

"I'll trailer in a couple of horses, and—''

"Horses?''

"For the ride.''

"Oh. That. Well. I thought you meant in a car...'' Cupid's voice faded.

"Cupid? You aren't scared of horses, are you?''

"Oh, no. I love horses. I just...''

"Yes?''

"I just had this crazy thought, that's all.''

"Are you going to tell me?''

She hesitated. "Lyrics. To that old song. The ones that go 'love and marriage, love and marriage, they go together like a horse and carriage.' I don't know what's wrong with me...it just seemed to fit.''

He paused, and a slow smile spread across his face. "Nothing's wrong with you, Cupid. Nothing at all.''

Cupid glanced at the clock again. She didn't think noon would ever roll around. It was the first time she could ever remember really being in a hurry to get out of the post office. Usually she dilly-dallied, straightening things up, making sure the floor was clean and the counters tidy. Today, she peered out onto the sidewalk, and seeing no one on the streets or headed in her direction, she locked up early. Five minutes early.

Five minutes closer to Burke Riley.

The thought took her breath away.

So did the guilt.

She hadn't seriously looked at so much as a boot scraper for him, let alone a bride. She meant to. She did. But there always seemed to be something wrong with everyone she thought of, and she rarely gave them more than two second's consideration. If she was going to do this right—especially for Burke—she wanted the match to be flawless.

The forever kind of love.

She took a deep breath, turned the brass lock on the post office door and silently chanted her personal mantra, *Smitten, with an arrow to the heart, lost forever to Cupid's dart.*

It was the best she could do for him, and she used it only in the most dire of cases.

Burke Riley, she'd concluded, was a dire case. He needed to be loved and cherished and transported to a new realm of existence. She could almost feel the potential waiting to be unleashed, as if he had a storm of emotion just waiting to be turned into tender thoughts and late-night passions.

She had even heard it in his voice last night, when he'd called. She'd detected a note of yearning she'd once thought he was too stubborn and stoic to reveal. It had been slight, but she had heard it. That was a good indicator.

It gave her a kind of heady exuberance to think that she could be the woman to bring him to his knees with love. Why, making a successful match for him would be the greatest feat of her matchmaking career. "Not a feather in the cap," as her mother fondly quoted, "but an arrow in the quiver."

It was strange, the infatuation Cupid had for Burke.

She thought of him all the time. She'd scanned his astrological charts and factored in his assessed compatibility potentials. The results weren't particularly stunning, but they were interesting…very interesting.

He definitely had a penchant for loyalty and commitment, but it would have to be triggered by the right woman.

The disturbing part was the suggestion that he could voluntarily insulate his heart. Stonewalling, they called it in the business.

It was mostly the big, strong, silent types that stonewalled. According to the Romantic Law of Averages and Statistics, a certain percentage of women were irresistibly attracted to the strong, silent type.

Cupid herself fell into that category. Probably because those were the most challenging of all men. They were often dark and brooding, like romantic heroes in the classics.

As for Burke, he made Cupid feel like she was floating. When she was near him, her heart seemed to soar and her spirit seemed to lift. Her mind did astonishing things, somersaulting into a mother lode of creative ideas—each and every one of them connected to Burke Riley. The man filled her with energy—sublime, irrepressible energy.

With him, Cupid had a distinct sense of the future. The picture was distorted, but it was bordered with roses. Red roses. Cupid's personal expression of love.

Cupid had experienced those borders on more than one occasion. But sometimes the roses were wilted, or thorny, or the image of falling petals blighted the vision. This time, however, they were bright and fresh. Dew-kissed.

Cupid had never experienced a feeling like that with

another human being in her entire life. It was intoxicating. And it also made her extremely wary.

Cupid owned a little bungalow on the south side of Valentine. Though it was a tract house, she'd made it into a charming home with paint. There were flower boxes beneath the two front windows, and a gated, white picket fence enclosed the front yard.

Burke, his pickup and his horse trailer were already at the end of her drive. The tailgate of the trailer was down, and a beautiful little horse with fine legs and a silky mane and tail nuzzled his shoulder. Cupid hurriedly parked her car and climbed out, wondering how much time she'd already missed with Burke.

"Well, like they say, we've come a long way, baby," Burke drawled, smiling at her.

The way he said it made Cupid want to melt. She liked that. No unnecessary 'hi, how are you?' Just that hint of familiarity, that flirtatious demeanor.

"And who do we have here?" she asked, extending a tentative hand to the horse Burke had on a lead.

"This here's Rosie," he said, stepping aside so she could make friends with the mare.

Cupid blinked numbly. Rational thought evaporated. "Rosie?"

"Her coloring," Burke explained unnecessarily. "For the fairest rose in all the land," he quipped.

Cupid forced a smile, yet the coincidence was unsettling. *A horse? She'd been dreaming about a horse?* Okay, her imagination, especially with red roses, was imprecise. "She's...lovely," Cupid managed to murmur.

Burke smiled broadly. "Figured she'd be a good fit

for you. Like you two were made for each other, with that red-blond hair and all.''

"Strawberry blond," Cupid said absently, stroking Rosie's nose.

"Mmm. A strawberry roan for a strawberry blonde."

Cupid sidled a look at Burke as his gaze drifted over her head. She experienced a ripple, as if he'd touched her. Immediately after that, she felt as if a steel rod shot up her spine, and she straightened. Absolutely no fraternizing, she reminded herself.

"So," she said carefully. "You put some thought into this. That's good to know. It could even be considered romantic, Burke. Some women would definitely appreciate that kind of attention."

"Think it'll win me points in the finding-a-wife department?"

"It could." Cupid combed Rosie's forelock with her finger.

"You going to set me up with any of your friends?"

Discomfort scuttled through Cupid. Why should she offer her friends *that* kind of favor? "Oh, no. Probably not. My friends are all rather farflung. Why, I'd have to drag you halfway across the country to arrange introductions. Everyone's doing this career thing, this see-the-world thing. Postponing marriage and a family is trendy right now."

Burke snorted. "Sure. Until they get to be my age, and then desperation sets in. They start wondering what they're missing. Or if they're going to be alone for the rest of their lives."

Cupid stared at him, her hand gripping Rosie's halter. "Do you really wonder what you're missing, Burke?"

He looked down at her with eyes that were curiously soft and warm. Then, just as quickly, a veil dropped over them, shutting out even the briefest glimpse of emotion. "I didn't mean me, exactly," he said evasively. "I just meant in general terms. These days it seems people live their lives, and go about their business, and no one's in a real hurry to find another person to spend their life with."

"Oh. Of course."

He affectionately brushed Rosie's nose away as she nuzzled his shoulder. "What?" he asked. "Didn't I give the right answer?"

Opening up was going to be hard for Burke; Cupid knew better than to push him. She just had this unnatural desire to know what was inside him, what made him tick. "I think, Burke Riley, that as male marriage material you have tremendous potential. I just..." Cupid paused, unconsciously gnawing her lower lip.

She looked up to see him watching her, the most mesmerized expression on his face. She stopped gnawing. Immediately. Lip nibbling could be perceived as an invitation and she simply could not risk inviting him any further into her life.

"I only want to get to know you better," she said instead. "So we can get you off on the right foot, with the right woman."

Burke grinned. It was an irresistible off-center smile that dimpled his sculpted cheeks. "Cupid," he said, amusement threading his deep, rich voice, "I get the feeling that this is a game to you. You don't put notches on your bedpost, do you? For getting people together?"

A slight flush crept into Cupid's cheeks. "Don't be silly," she exclaimed dismissively, glad he hadn't seen the quilt on her bed. Every heart she'd cross-stitched into it was dedicated to a couple she'd matched. "It's my name. It gives me more grief than you could know."

She feigned annoyance. "I thought you came out here to ride, and to talk about me helping you."

His grin faded into the nicest smile. "Okay. I don't intend to jeopardize the good thing I've got going." He skimmed his eyes down her length, taking in her postal worker's uniform. "Need to change?"

She lifted a shoulder. "Give me two minutes. Oh..." She looked at Rosie, then at his horse, which was still in the trailer. "Do you want to come in?"

He flicked a glance at the house, his eyes lingering on the paper valentines she'd recently taped in the windows. "No, I better take Archie out and get him saddled. We shouldn't waste a second of this good weather."

"I agree. It's incredible." Cupid lifted her arms and stretched, rolling her eyes heavenward. "No coat, and it's the middle of January. If I didn't know better I'd think..."

"Yes?"

"Um, that the Fates are smiling down on us," she said vaguely.

"The Fates?" He chuckled. "You really don't believe in that stuff, do you?"

"Me? Oh, no," she assured him, crossing her fingers behind her back. "Not at all."

# *Chapter Six*

The nice thing about living in small-town Kansas, Burke decided, was that no one looked twice when they rode their horses through the subdivision and onto the wide shoulder of Highway 63. They took the old road for a couple of miles, past the rock quarry.

Burke turned in his saddle. "The Windmill Tavern's up the road a bit. Want to stop?"

"Absolutely." Cupid stood in her stirrups and tried to get the kink out of her back. "Besides, the perfect woman may be up there, tending bar and waiting for a guy like you."

"You think so, huh?"

Cupid slipped back into the saddle and pulled her horse up alongside his. "Not really, but I thought it would make you happy to hear it."

He smiled at her, indulgently. "I thought we were going to talk about my messed-up wedding plans, but we've managed to dance around that."

"Ride," Cupid corrected. "We've ridden around that."

Burke shrugged and nudged his horse in the direction of the Windmill. Cupid did also, and they rode side by side on the shoulder of the blacktopped highway.

"I'd booked a trip to Las Vegas and reserved a wedding chapel. We agreed to get married quickly, so I figured if I got everything booked there'd be no changing our minds, no turning back."

"Just like that?" Cupid asked.

"Just like that. Reckoned I'd be married on February 14 this year."

The mere mention of the date made Cupid's breath clutch. February 14 for Cupid was comparable to Christmas for Santa Claus. That was *her* day. On that date, momentous things happened in her life.

She turned to Burke so quickly that her thigh brushed his knee. From the point of impact awareness radiated outward, prickling her nerve endings. She stared at him, experiencing myriad strange sensations and wondering what on earth he had done.

"Yes?"

"Just wondering. Why did you pick that date?"

"The hearts and flowers stuff. Figured a woman would like that."

"Oh. You only did it because you thought she'd like it. So, it wasn't…genuine?"

"As genuine as I could make it."

Cupid digested the information, and choked back a whisper of panic. Why should she care what Burke had planned with Moira? It was past history.

Yet something about it did matter. It mattered a lot.

His decisions reflected him, even if his answers sometimes distorted the picture. She had to know what made this man tick, what prompted his every move, his every decision. Apparently, he'd been prepared to indulge Moira just to get what he wanted. That was a little unsettling.

Unaware of Cupid's discomfiture, Burke reined Archie in at the gravel parking lot of the Windmill Tavern. He stopped beside the porch, near a half-filled water barrel, and swung down from the saddle.

Reins in hand, Burke moved around to look up at Cupid. "Need some help?"

The jaunty angle of his cowboy hat marked his features with arresting patterns of shadow and light. His shoulders seemed broader as if they could carry the weight of the world. As if they were prepared to protect and cradle, to hunch with love and intimacy. The evocative visions Cupid had of him were downright distressing. "I, uh…"

"Let me help," he offered, snagging her reins and extending his right hand. "I know you're not used to this."

Grasping the saddle horn, Cupid tentatively placed her other hand on his shoulder. Through his cotton shirt, she could feel the tension of hard-packed muscle, the warmth of flesh and the density of bone. It was unnerving, all of it, this closeness.

She flexed her knees to swing her leg over the back of the saddle, and felt the gentle pressure of his palm at her waist. His fingers curved around her rib cage. She slid slowly down, until one foot hit the ground, and then she pitched back against Burke, her other foot still in the stirrup.

"Sea legs," she said weakly, finally yanking her foot free and turning around.

"We get you riding," he said, "and in no time you'll be swaggering just like any old cowboy."

"Mmm. That would be attractive," she said, vaguely aware of being sandwiched between him and the creaking saddle he'd cinched on Rosie.

Burke glanced over her shoulder and frowned. Then he reached behind her, to give the saddle blanket a tug and straighten it. When he was finished his hand lingered there on the edge of the blanket.

Cupid was intimately enclosed by him. On all sides. The reins on one side, his arm on the other, the saddle at her back and his size and strength towering over her. It was a heady feeling, seductive, with the strangest feeling of trust thrown in.

For she did trust Burke. Implicitly.

"What do you think?" he asked, his head angling down to hers, a probing light in his eyes. "Is this a good way to spend a Saturday afternoon?"

"Yes," she said breathlessly. "The best."

"I should have figured this out years ago, instead of thinking Indian summers were for mending fence and cleaning stalls and hauling hay."

Archie pulled his head up from the water barrel, and Rosie nudged him aside, to move in for a drink. Space opened up behind Cupid, but she discovered to her surprise—and consternation—that she didn't want to move into it. Her body did not want to move an inch away from Burke's.

Burke fiddled with the two sets of reins and stayed rooted to the spot next to her. "I used to come here as a kid," he said.

"You did?"

"Mmm. It was one of my dad's favorite hangouts."

"Really? This is a long way from home."

Burke lifted a shoulder noncommittally. "Thurlby's a pretty dry town. And my dad claimed Niles and Clarkston were small places where small minds flourished. He liked to ranch, raise hell and keep his friendships fleeting."

"Is that one of the reasons you haven't spent more time around there, looking for a bride?"

Burke's eyes narrowed. "Most likely."

"I know they're small towns, but—"

"But they're filled with people who said, 'Stay away from Punch Riley's kid. Someday he's gonna take after his old man, and then there'll be hell to pay.'" Burke moved around the front of both horses and tied them to the corner post. "Didn't seem, with that kind of recommendation, that it was a real good place to find a wife. Reckoned it would be best for me to move away from Punch Riley's reputation."

Cupid didn't have to make any brilliant deductions. It was pretty obvious that Burke had been spurned as a child, and she guessed that's where a lot of his hurt came from.

Burke waited until the waitress had placed steaming cups of frothy cappuccino in front of them before he popped the question. "So. Be honest. Have you zeroed in on a bride for me?"

"Burke…" Cupid fiddled with the handle on the coffee cup, feigning great interest in turning it to the right angle. "I am working on it. But Valentine isn't that big of a place, either. The pickings around here are kind of slim."

"You're being too particular. Either that, or you aren't taking this seriously. C'mon. I figured by now you'd have found me at least a possibility. Someone."

"I'm taking this very seriously," she protested. "I've checked your astrological charts, biorhythms, compatibility potentials and—" Cupid gulped, realizing what she'd just admitted.

He leaned back, studying her. "You know, sometimes I don't know whether you're kidding or not."

She swallowed guiltily. "I wouldn't kid around about marriage, Burke. I only meant I might have to broaden my search. I know a lot of people," she said. "I just don't think any of them are quite right. Not for you."

He lifted an eyebrow, but kept his focus on the cappuccino. "I'm probably a hard fit. Folks see me as hard." *Yes. In every good sense of the word.* "Unforgiving." *Never that. Only a challenge.* "Short-tempered and antisocial." *A hungry man waiting to be fed, and tamed.*

He looked at her expectantly.

"Ah. I see," she said finally. "All the traits a good woman wants to fix. Hey, maybe I was wrong. This could be easier than I thought."

Burke's mouth quirked. He pensively folded a corner of the paper napkin over, then scraped the seam with his thumbnail. "I'll make you an offer," he said. "If you want to broaden your search, we'll take it out of state."

"Oh. Right."

"No. I'm serious. I've got the tickets for Las Vegas. We might as well use them. Four days, three nights in a luxury hotel. People just waiting to mingle and meet. Ought to be prime hunting grounds, the way I figure it."

Cupid hedged, the negative images coming first. Party girls. Down-on-their-luck women looking for another spin of the wheel. Old maid schoolteachers looking for a last-chance companion. Bored office workers whose only significant relationships centered around their computers. "I don't know. A visit, a vacation, that's one thing. But to find someone…there? No pun intended, but I think it would be a crap shoot."

Burke chuckled. "Okay. So we go for the visit and the good times. Whatever happens happens. Everything's paid for, so it's just like you said—if I find someone great. If not…" He lifted a shoulder.

Burke's relaxed demeanor allowed positive energy to flow into Cupid's brain. A multitude of people filled with hope, expectancy, waiting for someone to share the joy. Excitement and laughter, with a little longing thrown in. Women in sexy, appealing attire. Men in tuxedos. Singles, lots of them, looking for that perfect mate.

It could be a matchmaker's paradise. An opportunity Cupid might never have again.

"I've got the tickets, and you're invited," he wheedled.

"I do need a vacation," she conceded absently, "even if it would be a working vacation."

"A what?"

Burke's question jarred Cupid. "I—I meant that it's—it's usually hard work for me to take a vacation. On the spur of the moment like that. But I had to take the week off before Valentine's Day this year because my supervisor said my presence creates too much havoc in the post office."

"So you *could* go."

"Technically."

"Technically, hinging on what?"

"Well, if I wanted to, of course."

"Sounds like it's preordained, Cupid."

Cupid's breath caught in the back of her throat. The man couldn't have said anything more compelling if he'd planned it.

Seeing her flummoxed expression, Burke chuckled. "You know you want to. I can see it in your eyes."

Cupid's eyes widened. Well. If this wasn't a reversal. She was the one who was supposed to look into other people's eyes and discover the truth, and the inclination.

It didn't work this way. At least…it never had before.

She was treading on dangerous ground, deciding to spend a few days with him like that. But it would be for a good cause, and probably sanctioned. Making a match for Burke would be tantamount. It would bolster her resilience—as well as resistance—and it would hone her skills. She could learn far more from this experience than any other.

"You're right," she said carefully. "I do want to do it. And I will."

"That's my girl," Burke said encouragingly. He laid a hand on her wrist and gave it a comforting squeeze. "We leave in two weeks, and I'll make you a promise— I'm bringing home a wife."

# Chapter Seven

Cupid peeked in the back door of her parents' home. Her mother was in the kitchen, bending over the oven. Giving a quick rap on the door, to warn her she had company, Cupid walked right in. "Hi, Mom."

"Hi, honey." Venus stood, a tray of cookies in hand.

"You just got back yesterday, and you're already making cookies?" Cupid avoided the hot tray and managed to give her mom a quick hug.

"For the grandkids."

"Of course."

"Lysandra's got her hands full, and Valentine's Day is just around the corner. C'mon. You can help me frost them."

Cupid took off her coat and hung it on the back of a kitchen chair. She automatically sat down to the bowl of pink frosting and picked up one of the cooled, heart-shaped cookies. "How was your trip?"

"Wonderful. Saw people I haven't seen for years."

"And Daddy? What did he think?"

Venus paused, a spatula poised over the tray of cookies. A gleam came into her eye and a smile stole onto her face. She winked. "Oh, he found all that love and romance a real inspiration. Took twenty-five years off his age, I swear it did."

"Mom," Cupid warned, feeling a slight flush of discomfort.

"What? And you don't want to hear it, given your gift? Both my babies, gifted like that."

"Mmm. That's what I came to talk to you about. Specifically. My gift." Cupid swiped at one of the cookies with a glob of pink frosting and a butter knife.

Venus immediately dumped the emptied tray in the sink and came over to the chair opposite her daughter. "What? Is there a problem?"

"I sort of got myself a client." Cupid put down the frosted cookie and picked up another.

Her mother shrugged. "It happens."

"Well, I didn't mean for it to. But this guy came in the post office, thinking he was going to meet the mail-order bride of his dreams, and I gave her away. To someone else."

"Oh. The connection didn't fire, huh?"

"Nope. I made a huge boo-boo. I ended up stuck with him, and now I feel like I'm obligated or something."

"I see...."

"I'm having trouble with the calculated match. I've looked at it from every angle. Nothing seems right. Not for him."

"Mmm. Your sister—Lysandra?—she's the one to do a calculated match."

"Mom—"

"You? You're instinctual. When it comes to making

matches, you two girls are different as night and day. Always have been."

Cupid picked up another cookie, and instead of frosting it, put a dollop of frosting on the end and took a huge bite out of it. "That's not the problem," she said, licking a cookie crumb off her lower lip. "Not exactly. He wants me to go to Las Vegas with him, to find a wife. And I said yes."

"Oh. Personal involvement."

"I don't know what I was thinking."

"Cupid? I have the strangest feeling there's more to this than meets the eye."

Reminded of Burke's comment—*he could see it in her eyes*—Cupid winced. "It's...weird," she said finally, lifting both shoulders before slumping back against the chair. "He *reads* me. And he's right on target! I mean, I'm supposed to be the one reading him. It's gotten all messed up. And I'm not sure who's in control anymore."

"Ah. This is something new for you."

"Technically, I suppose, I could make him a match, and he could take *her* to Las Vegas."

"I suppose."

"But it just doesn't feel right."

"I understand, dear."

"But you know, Mom, I really want to go."

"So go." Her mother studied her perceptively. "You know, Cupid, your father reads me occasionally. It's never stopped me from having a good time. Or enjoying it. I think it's kind of...fair, actually."

"Fair? What's fair about it? I'm the one who's supposed to be pulling the strings in this department!"

"Cupid," her mother soothed, shushing her, "if he's

a good man, forget about it. You'll find a way to work around it. It just may not be the way you imagined things would turn out, that's all."

So. Cupid Jones was going to Las Vegas. With Burke Riley.

The entire premise was unnerving.

Her mother thought it was for the best, and had complacently encouraged her to have fun. Her father had slipped her a twenty and told her to put it all on number 14.

Burke was going to look for a wife, and for the life of her, Cupid didn't know why she was tagging along. Had she lost her ever-lovin' mind? Let him find his own wife and make his own mistakes! Why should she be subjected to this atrocity?

She'd talked on the phone with him every night for the last two weeks, and their conversations often drifted far afield from her finding him a wife. The more she learned about Burke, the more fascinated she'd become. The man was interesting. He had so much potential, so much verve, so much vitality. And he had awakened feelings in Cupid that she'd never before experienced.

Why would a man like this settle for a superficial marriage?

Why should he have to?

The man was marketable. Cupid could spout off Burke's marketability factors as easily as she could count to ten: he was likable, with high energy and good resources, not to mention solid, generous, amusing, kind, attentive, pleasant and intelligent. Plus he wasn't half-bad to look at.

As he stood at the ticket counter barely four feet in front of her, getting their boarding passes, she ran her gaze down his backside. All broad shoulders, clad in leather and lean, boot-cut denims. The heels of his boots were scuffed, but his black-banded Stetson looked brand-new.

In the old days, her mother would have referred to Burke as a "catch." Today, Cupid considered him a rare find.

Burke slung his carry-on bag over his shoulder and turned back to her. "All set," he announced, escorting her them away from the counter. "Cupid, what *are* you eating?" he asked, his expression suddenly quizzical.

"Soul food," Cupid automatically answered, fingering the candy in her pocket. "I get a little nervous before I fly."

"You eat soul food before a flight?"

"Want some?" Cupid paused midstride and extended her hand. On her open palm rested three candy hearts. Conversation hearts. A pink one, face side up, read Only You.

Cupid blanched.

Beside her, Burke paused to study the candies. "Figures," he said wryly. He reached between the two overturned white candy hearts to pluck the pink one from her palm. "Is this like reading tea leaves or cards or something? Or like having your palm read?"

"I think," Cupid said carefully, "it's the luck of the draw. Or a fluke." There was no way—none—that she could let Burke see how affected she was by this "random happening." There were no random happenings. There were only signs disguised by events. Cupid believed in signs and directions. She had been first in her class of Signs and Directions, at St. Valentine's Academy of Roses.

"Then there's no significance to this?" Burke arched a brow and popped the pink-tinted heart into his mouth.

Cupid went a little weak in the knees. She bore the involuntary reaction stoically and plastered a smile on her face. "It'll get you primed for a little romance. But that's about all," she quipped.

He grinned down at her, and without warning, a fleeting sense of longing nipped the corner of her heart.

Cupid, who was used to small buildings in a small town, found the sprawling immensity of Las Vegas incomprehensible. She stared at the four-story-high marble rotunda of the Oasis, the hotel Burke had chosen.

"Newest hotel on the strip," Burke said, before the desk clerk came to help him with checking in. "And I'd like to get another room for my traveling companion," he requested, handing the young woman his credit card. "If we could get adjacent rooms, or something on the same floor—"

"I'm sorry, sir. We're completely booked."

Burke's hand stilled. "But you've got thousands of rooms."

"Three thousand, four hundred and fourteen," the woman said proudly. "And all of them are booked. The dental convention's in town." She reached for a listing of phone numbers. "I've heard the Taj may have rooms. It's about seven blocks away, but I can try to get you an extra room there."

Burke shot a questioning glance in Cupid's direction.

"Seven blocks?" she repeated. "That will be kind of inconvenient."

The desk clerk checked her computer screen. "It says here you've booked a bridal suite..." She looked from Cupid to Burke.

"There's been a change of plans," Cupid said hastily. "With the wedding night."

"Oh. I see." The desk clerk sent Burke a pitying glance. It was clear she didn't see at all.

He coughed loudly.

"Well, it is a suite," the desk clerk continued. "There'd be room for a roll-away cot, if I can scare one up."

Heat crawled up the back of Cupid's neck, but she refused to give in to the awkwardness of the situation.

"I'm sorry, darling," Burke began, playing the role of the patient groom to the hilt. "I never thought, in a place this big..."

Cupid brushed off the apology. "It's okay. We can make do. I mean, it's not like we'll be suffering or anything."

"I'll make it up to you." He hung an arm around her shoulder and drew her next to him.

"It's okay. Really. It won't hurt us to share a room," she said, trying to put a little distance between them.

*It wouldn't hurt? Really?*

The clerk handed Burke two card keys, then hesitated. "You know, when clients book a bridal suite we assume they want it immediately...but, to make up for the mis-understanding, over the availability of rooms and all, I've arranged to provide you with a complimentary mid-night massage. It's something special for newlyweds. You can book it whenever you like."

"Oh!" Cupid protested. "No—"

"Thank you," Burke interjected, swiping the cards and the certificate from her hand. "That's very thought-ful of you."

"What are you doing?" Cupid muttered, as they walked to the elevators.

"Figure as long as I'm doing this I might as well go whole hog. For me and my bride."

The way he said it, so possessively, made Cupid feel a little bit left out. As if she was missing out on something—some intimacy due her.

Right now, however, his confident attitude rankled her. Instead of feeling anticipation at the prospect of finding him a bride, she felt like a voyeur. She didn't want to know too much about Burke and his soon-to-be Mrs. She couldn't bear it. She didn't want to admit his life would move on, in a different direction—a direction that didn't include her.

Sure, she'd miss him, but there should be some consolation in knowing she would continue to do the same things—matchmaking in working at the post office, attending everyone's weddings. She should feel some satisfaction in that...but she couldn't. She just couldn't.

They waited in the lobby for a free elevator. "What floor is the room on?" Cupid asked, trying to focus on something sensible, something in the here and now.

"Mmm..." Burke scanned the card. "The fourteenth."

Cupid swiveled her head. "You can't be serious?" she said without thinking.

He tipped the card in her direction, so she could see for herself.

"That's *my* number!" She explained in disbelief.

"So you told me. And I have to say that it does keep popping up a lot around you."

A new wave of desperation crept over Cupid. "But, hey, this is a big hotel, right? They have a lot of rooms. I mean, as luck would have it—"

The elevator doors opened like a yawning chasm, waiting to take her to the fires of hell—or to the feverish throes of the heavenly bridal chamber.

Burke waited until the doors closed and they were

alone in the elevator. He pushed the button for the fourteenth floor, then turned to Cupid. "Are you nervous about this?" he asked.

She fingered the candy conversation hearts in her pocket. "Me?" The word came out as a little squeak, and she cleared her throat. "Of course not."

His gaze, dead serious, raked over her. "Nothing's going to happen that you don't want to have happen."

It was on the tip of her tongue to deny that anything would happen…but she couldn't bring herself to utter it. Because her mind had already fast-forwarded into what it would be like to share the pleasure, the pure exhilaration, of being alone with Burke in the same suite, sharing the midnight massage, or the token bottle of champagne.

Cupid looked away, grateful the doors of the elevator opened just then. "I know," she said evenly. "I wouldn't be here if I didn't trust you."

"This isn't about trust, Cupid."

She stopped cold.

He glanced down at her, indicating she should precede him into the hall. "It's more than that," he said, his eyes flicking to the brass room plates. "I think you're really here because you can't resist doing me a favor. There's something about you… You just can't help yourself when it comes to doing things for other people. I really like that about you."

"You do?"

"Yeah. I doubt there's a handful of people in the world who would bother," he said cynically. "I wouldn't."

His response confused her, making her wonder once more if she'd misjudged him. "But…you were the one who asked me to find you a bride."

"No. I told you." He paused at the room, dismissing the matter. "Here. I think this is it." He inserted the card into the lock and pushed the door open.

Cupid gasped. The room was like nothing she'd ever seen in her entire life. Amazed, she stood still and gazed at the amenities. Red roses in a lead crystal vase on a black onyx table. Champagne chilling on ice, next to the black leather couch in front of the gas fireplace. A panoramic vista of the sprawling city of Las Vegas.

A massive heart-shaped bed, decked out in red silk sheets and piped in black satin, stood twenty feet away, on a raised platform that ran from wall to wall. Yards and yards of pouffed tulle, held by narrow red and black ribbons, created a headboard effect, while a half-dozen throw pillows, in satin and lace, were piled at the head of the bed. Black satin pajamas, embroidered His and Hers, were artfully arranged at the foot.

Cupid stared at them, and her heart started thrumming, imagining what it would be like to slip into identical sleepwear. Imagining a midnight massage, where only black satin and Burke's work-roughened hands caressed her body. She shivered.

Burke followed her gaze—and promptly diverted her attention. "Let's look at the bathroom," he said, tossing open the door.

Cupid stared into a cavern of black marble, mirrors and gold fixtures. The bath was an adult's playground. The heart-shaped whirlpool tub wasn't intended for bathing—it was intended for a good romp. Beyond, the shower beckoned, the view distorted by glass block walls. Cupid guessed it was bigger than her galley kitchen. It even had bench seating! On the counter, between the twin lavatories, mounds of fluffy black towels stood next to sample packets of massage oils and creams.

"Well, this is...decadent," she said finally.

"What's your favorite flavor?" Burke asked, picking up the basket of oils.

"Excuse me?"

"We have raspberry, lemon, honey and oatmeal. Uh-oh. Check this out. Cherries and chocolate."

Cupid grimaced. "Sounds more like a buffet."

"And last, but not least, is...steamin' strawberry, from—" Burke stopped and swallowed a belly laugh "—from Cupid's Den."

"You're making this up!"

"Swear to God, I'm not!"

He tilted the foil packet her direction, and Cupid wilted. "This is tacky. Just tacky. Love and romance is getting all mixed up with tacky commercialism. I mean, c'mon. Wedded bliss has been reduced to foil packets of massage oil, and silks and satins, and whirlpool jets and, and—"

"Champagne in the firelight," he supplied. "To be shared on leather couches made for two."

Cupid caught her breath. To hear him phrase things that way, his husky voice painting pictures in her mind, gave her pause. "I only meant, it's kind of insulting, my name being on something like that."

"I think it's kind of sexy." He pulled the packet out of the basket.

"You do?"

"Um-hmm. Steamin' Strawberry. Reminds me of you." His eyes lit up. "This sexy, indignant little package of promises." He handed it to her. "For you. Like you. Because of you. Keep it. A memento of our first night together."

She automatically accepted the packet, unaware it would be warm from his touch. Her fingers curled around it, aching to savor as much of his heat as she could. "If I didn't know better, I'd think you were flirting with me over this. Over our—"

"Don't," he interrupted her, chuckling. "I know what you're going to say, Cupid."

"What?"

"Over our *only* night together."

# Chapter Eight

They ate in the hotel, in a cozy little nook the concierge had reserved for them.

In the far corner, a strolling violinist played, his soulful music setting the mood. Cupid fingered the white linen tablecloths, and over the flickering candlelight, studied Burke's expression. "I never expected it to be like this."

He raised an eyebrow at the same time he raised his glass of wine. "You expected…?"

"A lot of noise. And people."

"We can find that." He took a sip of the wine. "If you want."

"No. I only meant this is so secluded. Intimate."

"It wasn't my idea to spend my honeymoon around a lot of people," he said, setting the wineglass aside.

"And instead you're spending it with me."

His silver gaze darkened, and tarnished. "There could be worse things."

Cupid had the distinct impression Burke intended the statement as a compliment.

"Good evening," the maître d' interrupted, "I'm in charge of the Oasis wait staff, and I wanted to make a stop and welcome you. We hope you're finding everything to your satisfaction. We like to make sure our newlyweds are happy."

"Oh, we're not—" Cupid began.

"Yes. Everything's fine," Burke said smoothly.

The maître d' didn't appear to hear Cupid's protest. "Good," he said pleasantly. "Well, I come bearing gifts from the management. A little token of our appreciation, and a little memento for you." He handed Cupid a long-stemmed red rose. "With our best wishes."

"Thank you," she murmured. *Another one.* Of course, she reasoned, it *was* traditional, and it was close to Valentine's Day.

"And for you, sir..." the maître d' handed Burke a silver frame "...a little remembrance."

Cupid leaned close, against his shoulder, to read the inscription on the bottom corner.

*Always.*

Cupid guessed, by Burke's taut reaction, that he didn't quite know what to do—or say—either.

"If you would look up, please? And smile..."

They looked up, into the startling flash of the cameras.

"Beautiful!" The maître d' beamed. "We'll deliver the portrait to your room. And may I say, congratulations. You do make a lovely couple."

The photographer and the maître d' made their exit as quickly as they had approached. Burke looked like he had been left holding the bag. He did, to put it succinctly, look like he had been framed.

Even though she felt like a fraud, Cupid's mouth began to wobble. She dragged the rose beneath her nose, to cover her amusement. "You should have told him the truth," she admonished.

Burke shook his head and strangled over a half laugh. "I was just going to say everything was fine, and send him on his way. No need going into all these explanations."

"I understand. For the life of me, I don't know what you're going to do with that frame, though."

"I do. I'm going to put our picture in it."

Cupid had a sinking feeling. She was doomed, there were no two ways about it. "Um, Burke. About that picture…"

"Yes?"

"That may not be such a good idea."

"Why not?"

She didn't want to go into detail. Not now. Maybe she could find a way to waltz around it. "Because you're looking to get married. To someone else," she said pensively. She avoided his gaze by tracing a rose petal with the tip of her fingernail. "And sometimes, like right now, I get the strangest feeling about the way things have turned out. Like I've taken something away from Moira. Like I'm filling in for what should have been her night, her honeymoon."

"Forget Moira. She wouldn't have appreciated tonight, anyway. Not like you do."

"But…I'm holding her rose. I'm enjoying her candlelit dinner for two. I'm sharing her bed—your bed," she clarified hastily. "Well, not technically, of course. Not with the cot coming, but—"

"Actually, you are," Burke said, without batting an

eye. "Sharing my bed, that is. The front desk called while you were in the shower. They weren't able to come up with a roll-away."

Cupid had been blindsided. No argument there. Had all her powers, including her sixth sense, gone on vacation? Or taken a leave of absence?

She intentionally let her gaze drift over to the empty silver picture frame Burke had propped on the mantel, and the inscription seemed to wink at her.

Always.

She should have known. She absolutely should have known.

At least awareness hadn't taken flight. She could feel Burke behind her, at her shoulder. His breath was warm against her neck.

"Cupid," he said gently, his fingertips resting just above her elbows, "I'll take the couch, you can have the bed. All to yourself."

"Don't be silly," she heard herself say. "I trust you to stay on your side of the bed. And I trust myself to stay on mine. We may as well be comfortable. How am I going to introduce you to anyone tomorrow if you look like you've been dragged through a knothole backward?"

A low rumble of appreciative laughter sounded from Burke's throat. It was the kind of husky male sound that made women swoon.

Cupid herself took a ragged breath. She hoped he'd refuse her offer, but he didn't.

"There's something about that bed that sort of pushes people together, don't you think?"

With her back against his chest, Cupid was grateful he couldn't see her eyes drift closed. "It wouldn't work that way for me, Burke…so don't even go there," she warned.

He made another low, throaty sound. "Mmm. And why not?"

"Because I don't take these things lightly."

"Oh. I see."

He loosened his grasp, and she detected disappointment. "I don't want to give you the wrong impression."

"You haven't."

"I didn't want you to think I'd just fall into bed with you," she said quickly. "I'm here to find you a wife, so it would complicate things if we got to know each other on any other level."

"Cupid? You ever slept side by side with a man?"

"Burke," she hedged, "I just said—"

"Slept," he repeated. "There's something very comforting about it. Hearing a woman's even breathing. Seeing the way her lashes lie across her cheek in sleep. The way her nightgown slips over her shoulder." Cupid's heart thudded against her chest. Burke Riley was a romantic—only he didn't even know it. "I imagine you must see the same kinds of sexy things, appealing things, about a man."

"Hold it. We're not talking about me here," she protested. "We're talking about you, and I thought you were getting married to find out about those things."

He chuckled confidently. "Getting married doesn't mean I haven't had my experiences. I know what it's like waking up next to a woman."

"Yes, well, I don't really need to know how you feel about something like that. That comes later, when I'm out of the picture." To emphasize her point, she put the picture frame face down on the mantel.

He laughed, the sound reverberating against her ear.

"You don't want to talk about it," he said perceptively. "I'll bet it's because you're a bed hog."

Cupid smiled in spite of herself. When they were growing up, Lysandra had always complained about Cupid hogging the blankets.

It was amazing. Burke had an incredible ability to make her laugh. He may have his faults, but he also had a soft side.

"Well, I thought maybe I'd go down for a paper or something."

"A paper?" Cupid glanced at the clock. "It's midnight."

"Okay. It's an excuse," he admitted. "Figured you'd like some time to get settled. For bed?"

Cupid's mouth formed a small, round O.

"Fifteen minutes?"

"Yes. Fine. I suppose you don't want me to use those black silk thingies." She inclined her head to the embroidered nightwear.

He chuckled. "Do whatever you want." He left immediately, and for an instant Cupid missed the warmth at her shoulder. He offered something akin to comfort, even when a lot of mixed-up feelings were assailing her.

Cupid knew she should hurry, but something made her dawdle. She brushed, washed and moisturized. Then, for some inexplicable reason, she put a swipe of mascara over her lashes. Looking into the mirror, she patted her cheeks, trying to put a little more color into her complexion.

"Well," she muttered, knowing full well she was making excuses, "I don't want him to wake up next to me and be completely disappointed."

She walked out into the suite, startled to see Burke

standing next to the fireplace, a folded paper in his hand. He turned, and their gazes collided.

"Sorry. I guess I didn't give you enough time," he said, staring at her, before his gaze drifted lower, to the thin straps of her nightwear.

Cupid wore the sheerest nightgown, a frothy garment with hearts splashed all over it, in shades of rose and wine. Beneath the hem, Burke glimpsed slim ankles and tiny feet. For some crazy reason, he imagined her pink-painted toes burrowing into the sheets—or nudging him during the night. To save himself, he banished the idea from his head. "I figured you'd be in bed, with the covers up to your chin."

"Ah, yes…that would be me, Little Red Riding Hood, waiting for the big, bad wolf," she teased.

She moved as if on autopilot toward the heart-shaped bed. It was a step up, as if it were on a pedestal.

Burke watched her remove some of the fancy pillows and start to turn down the bedspread. "Uh-oh," she said. "There are chocolates on the pillow. Want yours?"

It was the window of opportunity Burke had subconsciously been looking for. He moved toward Cupid, absently putting the paper on the marble table. "What's this? My midnight treat?"

As he asked the question, Cupid leaned over to pick up the foil-wrapped chocolates. He memorized her lithe movements, noting how fluidly she bent at the waist, watching the sweep of her arm, the tilt of her shoulder. Her short-cropped hair appeared wispy against the full, arching column of her neck, and a backdrop of light silhouetted the curve of her jaw, her chin, the tip of her nose.

When she straightened, he was beside her.

The thin spaghetti strap of her nightgown had shifted,

straggling over her shoulder. Cupid was apparently unaware of it.

Burke glimpsed the full rise of her creamy soft breasts, and the shadowy depression between. Then he noticed something else: a curious heart-shaped mark, the color of strawberry.

She extended the chocolates to him, and instead of accepting them, he reached instinctively to brush the pad of his thumb over the slightly raised flesh. "Birthmark?" he asked.

Cupid wrenched back, her head jerking as if she'd been shot. A short, gasping moan escaped her mouth, and she shuddered involuntarily. Burke steadied her, his arm beneath her elbow.

"Cupid...?"

"Don't ever—*ever*—do that again," she warned. Her hand, the one with the chocolates, hastily inched the strap of her nightgown up into place. "It's my sensitive spot," she explained, "my lovelorn Achilles' heel."

"Your what?"

Cupid looked surprised, as if she'd revealed something she hadn't intended. "Nothing. Just a saying, that's all." She pinned the nightgown into place with her fingertips, as if she were momentarily debating. "Some people are ticklish. I'm ticklish...there. On my shoulder."

"Huh. You're putting me on."

"No."

He stared at her, then he laughed. He guffawed, actually. "So you've got a birthmark. It's nothing to be ashamed of."

"I'm not ashamed of it," she retorted. "I'm proud of it. It's me! It's who I am."

He chuckled. "Okay, I didn't mean to tickle you."

"You didn't tickle me!"

"I didn't tickle you?"

"I meant—"

"Yes?"

"It's a sensitive spot. I don't let people go around poking my—my…"

"Yes?"

"My private parts!"

Burke snorted. God, he enjoyed her when she got like this. All het up, and indignant. "It was your shoulder. And it was exposed. There wasn't anything private about it."

"It's my sweet spot!"

"Excuse me?"

Cupid winced. "It's a family thing," she finally said dismissively. "One of those things that gets handed down through the generations."

"Like red hair, and a heart-shaped face?"

"I suppose."

"And a hand-me-down affection for all these hearts and flowers?" Burke asked softly. He snagged the spaghetti strap of her gown and pensively rubbed it between his forefinger and thumb.

Cupid squirmed, but she didn't back down. "You noticed?"

"And a longing to play matchmaker?" he asked, softer still.

"Exactly. You've got me and my gene pool all figured out."

"Oh, I see…you and your whole family are sitting out in western Kansas, plotting romance and making matches."

"To tell you the truth, my father isn't in the business."

The way she said it, so honest and straightforward, he almost believed that part of the fabrication. He stopped, then laughed at himself. "Okay. Enough. Give it to me straight. Are you really 'Cupid'?"

"Actually, Burke," she said slowly, "I am."

His mouth twitched. "You're telling me the truth?"

"Cross my heart." She made a little X over the swell of her breast.

He smiled broadly. Damn, she was good. "I should have known."

"Yes. You should have. I thought I was going to have to tell you, but you figured it all out. At least you saved me the trouble."

He laughed again, appreciatively. The strap slipped from his grasp and he couldn't help himself, he traced her jawline with his fingertip. "You are incredible, you know that?"

He found himself looking down, straight into her bow-shaped mouth. Memories of the time he had kissed her on the front steps of the Swingin' Door still haunted him. She was so sweet, so vulnerable…so very kissable. "You forgot the chocolates," he said thickly.

"Oh, they're…" she lifted them carefully, as if not wanting to break the slight physical contact between them "…probably melted."

He inclined his head. "Chocolate's best that way." He reluctantly pulled his hand away to accept the proffered sweet. She'd already peeled away the foil wrap. He waited until she tasted her piece, then he did the same, letting it dissolve on his tongue.

"One more thing," he proposed, "since you're turning back the sheets…?"

"Yes?"

"A good-night kiss?" The suggestion took her completely off guard; he could see it in her eyes. Burke didn't give her time to refuse. He wanted to taste the chocolate on her tongue almost as much as he wanted to feel her nightgown slide over her waist, her lower back, her hip.

His arm looped around her, drawing her to him. Her breasts flattened against his chest, and for one insane moment he was conscious of that crazy birthmark, and wondered if it was the lifeline to her heart.

He could have sworn the neckline of her gown shifted, allowing the strawberry-red spot to scorch him. Some intense reaction vibrated through his bones, and his belly went white-hot, his blood fiery.

It took an iron will to control the kiss, to keep it chaste. He wanted more, he definitely wanted all of Cupid…but he'd promised her she could trust him, and no matter what, he couldn't forget that.

# *Chapter Nine*

After the mind-boggling kiss, Burke matter-of-factly set her away from him.

Then, working the buttons as if he were on speed-dial, he stripped off his shirt and shrugged out of it. He tossed it on a nearby chair.

"What are you doing?" she asked shakily.

"Me?" His fingers paused on the brass button of his jeans. "I'm getting ready for bed."

Cupid, knowing she couldn't shed the what-do-I-do-next look from her face, whirled and dived between the covers and made a show of rearranging them.

Burke moved around the bed, to the other side. "I only wear my skivvies to bed. I hope that doesn't bother you."

"Oh, no. Not at all." Did her voice sound thin?

Burke popped the button on his jeans, and the waist-band sagged, revealing a snippet of milky white flesh at his hip. Then he turned his back to her. Cupid scrinched her eyes tightly closed. Doing so didn't banish the image of the muscled six-pack riding across his flat belly, or the bow-shaped spread of his bare shoulders.

She heard the rasp of his brass zipper, and the brush of denim being pushed down. He sat heavily on the bed beside her. She could feel him kicking off his boots, and socks and jeans. There were a couple of thumps and she imagined the tangle of clothes at his bedside.

Okay, he was messy. Concentrate on that, she told herself. Concentrate on anything other than the scent of his aftershave, the whisper of the sheets against his backside. His heavy, even breathing.

Using the remote control beside the bed, Burke clicked off the lights, and behind Cupid's eyelids, everything went blue-black and starry. Even so, she held her breath as he eased into bed.

Her eyes inched open, and she saw him settle onto his back, the covers over his chest. He stacked his hands behind his head and faced the ceiling.

"You going to go to sleep right away?" he asked.

"Um, probably not."

"Me, either. I can't believe I'm really here."

"*You* can't?"

He chuckled. "The trip caught you by surprise, did it, Cupid?"

"Right now, I should be hand-canceling envelopes with a stamp that says Delivered with Love, from Valentine, Kansas."

He snorted. "You enjoy your job?"

"I guess."

"That doesn't sound like an endorsement."

"I like certain things about it. The people, the hours, the paycheck. But there's a part of me that's a homebody. I wish I had more hours to bake cookies, or plant more flowers, or—I don't know, that kind of stuff."

It was the strangest thing; Cupid was certain she could feel Burke smiling.

"You know what's missing in this room?" he said finally.

"What?"

"Stars on the ceiling."

Cupid turned her head, not sure she'd heard him correctly.

"Oh, this city has a lot of lights, but they're all artificial. You can't see the sky. Not at night."

"And plastic stars on the ceiling would help?"

"For me, I guess."

They lapsed into silence, considering.

She felt, rather than saw, Burke shift his position. "You know, I've got an extra, empty arm, if you want to get comfortable."

A second of silence slipped away. "I won't be violating any trust if I do that, will I?"

"Nah. We could look up at our little piece of blue-black heaven together." Cupid didn't reply, but she moved closer, putting her head in the crook of his elbow. Her shoulder brushed the wall of his chest. "That better?" he asked.

"Yes. Fine."

"You sure?" He adjusted his arm slightly. "I don't want to bump your, um, sweet spot, and hurt you or anything."

Cupid smiled, wishing she'd never mentioned that. There'd probably be penance to pay. "You won't hurt me, Burke."

"You're sure about that?"

"Oh. I'm pretty confident."

They endured another stretch of silence, of awareness. Burke's body cradled her, in the most intimate way. Her ears, always acute, detected the beat of his heart. Her nape recognized the sinew cording of his arm; her shoulder snuggled against his side.

"Tell me about your ranch," she said.

He did. He told her everything.

How his dad had built the house in the fifties, a rambling brick affair with more bathrooms than bedrooms, and a sunporch that sizzled in the summer and was downright arctic in the winter. He told her about the shorthorns he raised, and the quarter horses he bred.

In the darkness, his voice became intoxicating, passionate, about the life he had fashioned for himself.

He talked about the hard work, but even that, the way he described it, carried an appeal. He talked about the two hands he had working for him year-round—Brendon, a sheep rancher from Australia, and Lester, a grizzled old cowpoke from the Montana high country.

He even told her about his mother. She'd remarried an academic—a professor who wore brown tweed sport coats with leather patches on the elbows, and who came from old money. They had spent the last six years in the Philippines. Burke heard from her twice a year, once on his birthday and once at Christmas.

He even talked about painting the kitchen, in anticipation of Moira's arrival. He'd intended it to be sunrise peach; it had turned out pretty damn pink.

Cupid laughed. "I can see it now. Big, bad Burke Riley, frying up eggs in a pink kitchen."

He snorted. "Lay off. The color kind of grows on you."

"You make it—all of it—sound wonderful. I'd like to see it someday."

"I imagine you will, Cupid. Someday."

* * *

Cupid woke and inched nearer the tantalizing source of heat. Burke.

She stretched and lazily rolled on her side to peek at him. His cheeks and chin were the texture of coarse sandpaper. Yet the hard angles and planes of his features were relaxed, and the cleft above his brow had disappeared. In sleep, his breathing was even, rhythmic.

Cupid quietly pushed the sheets down and started to get up. A hand clamped over her wrist, stopping her.

"Where are you going?" he asked thickly.

"I'm going to get dressed. We have a long day ahead of us."

"Mmm. Wife-shopping."

Her heart grew heavy. "Yes. Wife-shopping."

"We're just looking, aren't we? Like window shopping."

A smidgen of hope surfaced in Cupid. Maybe he really didn't want to go through with this. Maybe he'd realized that this wasn't the way to go about finding your life's mate. "What do you mean?"

"Oh, I don't know. I figured we'd go out today, see the lay of the land and then get serious."

"We can do that." She reluctantly gave her wrist a little tug, and he released her. Cupid pulled her most comfortable outfit out of the closet, then grimaced at the heart appliqué on the right sleeve. Burke would say something about it, she knew he would.

She hurried through her morning ritual, then rolled her sleeves up, so the appliqué didn't show, and came out to find Burke fully dressed, a bemused expression on his face.

"Check this out," he said, holding up an envelope. "Our picture, and a note from the management."

"Oh? Let me see." Though she feigned innocence, trepidation coursed through her.

"They've offered us complimentary dinner in the Solarium again tonight, and want to retake the photo. They said they couldn't get this curious red haze out." He tilted the glossy photo for her inspection.

"Hey, it must have been me," she shrugged, opting for that old joke. "I probably broke the camera."

Burke scuffed at it with his thumbnail. "That's strange. It's almost like red cigarette smoke floating over your head."

"I don't smoke," she reminded him. "Probably a phenomenon. Like steam from the buffet table or the kitchen or..."

He looked at her suspiciously. "We were in the corner, on the other side of the restaurant, in the nonsmoking section."

"Cheap film," she suggested.

Her explanation gave him pause.

"It's not a big deal," she said. "You'll probably find someone else and won't even want me in that photo—and certainly not sharing that picture frame with you."

He lowered the picture and his eyes narrowed thoughtfully. "Yes...well, let's be off, shall we? We can think about this later." He glanced back at the picture again. "It is a good picture of us, though. Even with all this red, misty stuff swirling around."

Cupid lifted both shoulders, as if the matter was truly of little consequence. "Hey, it's one of a kind."

"I know what it was," he joked. "You were probably seeing red, because the maître d' thought we were married."

"Oh, that's it. Yes, exactly that."

They both laughed easily, and Cupid was just as relieved when Burke dropped the photo on the side table and grabbed his jacket. "Ready?"

"Absolutely. Let's set this town on its ear."

He smiled broadly and opened the door for her. Cupid walked through ahead of him, aware that Burke was a thoughtful man in so many ways. She noticed he had a tendency to look after her, to see that she was comfortable, or if there was anything she needed. A good trait in a man, to be sure. Especially one who intended to marry.

For that was what it was about, really, Cupid often thought. Putting someone else first in your life.

They explored the hotels and gambling casinos, dropping quarters in slots when the spirit moved them, and checking out the entertainment, shops and attractions. They had so much fun together they both overlooked the real purpose of their trip.

It was late in the afternoon when Burke burrowed down into his jeans pocket, to fish out another quarter. "We haven't been very lucky today," he said ruefully, offering Cupid the warm quarter. "It's my last one."

An older, gray-haired man propped on a stool beside them laughed. "Haven't hit any big jackpots yet?"

Cupid inclined her head. "Nothing to write home about."

"Here," he said. "I'll match that, kids…and double it." Reaching into his cup of coins, he snagged a handful of quarters and dropped them into Cupid's hands.

"Oh, no. I couldn't," she protested.

"Go on. It's only money. Only a way to waste time."

"Thank you, but—"

"We're really not here to gamble," Burke explained. "This was supposed to be a honeymoon trip."

"Oh, well, congratulations, then!" The man stuck out his hand.

Cupid stood back, guessing it would be futile to explain that she was there only to recruit the intended bride.

"Sure do envy you. Starting out a life together," the gentleman admitted. "My missus passed on two years ago. Not much to do for an old duffer like me, not without someone to share things with. So I travel a bit now and then, just to fill up the days. The name's Vince McCoy. Glad to know you."

Cupid moved to drop the quarters back into Vince's cup.

"No, no," he protested. "Consider 'em a gift. Maybe Lady Luck will smile down on you and you'll find your pot of gold at the end of the rainbow."

Taking the quarters under the presumption they were honeymooners made Cupid uneasy...but there was something about the way he phrased his words that bothered her more. She detected a message. *A hidden message.*

"I'll buy them from you," Burke offered, pulling out his wallet.

"Forget it. You kids enjoy yourself. Why, this is the best time of your life."

Cupid got a very good feeling about Vince McCoy. A very good feeling, indeed.

She detected Vince's loneliness, and knew it was genuine. Giving him the once-over, she took in his green Colorado State polo shirt, his gold watch and signet ring.

Burke chatted with him briefly while Cupid's brain churned busily. She was inclined to find the kind old man a little happiness. It was the right thing to do.

"Yes, sir, now Colorado, that's God's country,"

Vince proclaimed. "Best thing that ever happened to me when I got offered that job at Colorado State."

Bells started ringing, and Cupid looked up between the rows of slot machines. Everything dulled—the sights, the sounds, the smells—as a rhinestone pin flashed, capturing her attention. Fashioned to spell Colorado State, the pin was attached to the white bodice of a silky dress shirt. A woman's perfectly coiffed hair, in arresting shades of pearl and platinum, floated over the machine behind them.

Cupid honed in, engaging the power of suggestion.

In seconds the trim, older woman came around the machine and moved into their aisle. "My..." She offered them a warm smile. "This is one busy place. I can't find a free machine anywhere."

"Take ours," Cupid invited, coaxing Burke off the stool.

"Are you sure? I don't want to take your place." She looked from them to Vince.

"Please," Burke said, "take it."

"So you're from Colorado?" Cupid asked.

"Graduated from Colorado State years ago," she said, "but I live in Tucson now. After my husband died, I said I was moving back. I guess I just need a reason."

Vince tapped his embroidered shirtfront. "I'm a transplant, but I'm *never* leaving," he declared.

The conversation immediately escalated for the older folks, into all the things they had in common. Burke chatted with them for a few moments, then motioned to Cupid, indicating they should make an exit.

But Cupid put a hand to his chest, stopping him. "No. Just a minute," she whispered, then turned to the woman. "And your name is...?"

"I'm June. June Whitley."

"June, I'd like to introduce you—officially—to Vince McCoy. Vince…" Cupid's voice went low, magnetic "…meet June."

They shook hands. Then—*ping!* the electricity of that first touch was palpable, and Cupid immediately glimpsed the glow of love in their eyes. It was corny, but in this business, that was how things happened. An introduction, a look, a handshake…and they were head-over-heels in love.

Burke and Cupid faded from the couple's perception.

"Well, we'll see you two then," Cupid said cheerily. "Have a nice life." Reaching for Burke's arm, she led him away.

He stumbled slightly, looking over his shoulder at Vince and June. "Did you see that?" he inquired. "I'd swear that looked like love at first sight."

"I thought you didn't believe in love at first sight." Cupid kept walking.

"I don't."

"Okay, then they're just two Colorado State fans who found each other."

"No…" He shook his head, obviously struggling to make sense of what he'd just witnessed. "We were talking football, and then they looked into each other's eyes…and it was like—like you and I dropped off the planet."

"You're exaggerating."

"Cupid. They didn't even know we were there. They didn't even know we left."

"It's really nice to see people bond like that, isn't it?" she said, with forced nonchalance.

Burke caught up with her, matching his steps to hers. They walked out of the hotel casino and onto the crowded sidewalk. "It's almost like you made that happen," he accused. "Like you *orchestrated* that. And *orchestrated* is not a word I use very often."

Cupid laughed. "Let me guess. It's a word your mother would use."

"She would." He sighed, and they automatically started walking toward the heart of the Las Vegas strip. "Now," he said, his gaze settling on a trio of women ahead of them, "if I were to suggest that woman in the green skirt as a possible candidate for me, what would you say about her?"

Cupid appraised the two shopping bags she carried. They were stuffed with plush animals and plastic toys. "My guess is she's a single mom...and she overindulges her children. It would be an issue."

"That one. In the blue."

Cupid took in the multiple rings on her fingers, the chains and charms around her neck, the stack of bracelets on her arm. "Self-absorbed. She'd frustrate you."

"That woman with the yellow cap."

Cupid considered the running shoes, the hooded sweatshirt and sweatpants. "A gym fanatic. It would never work."

Burke grumbled in exasperation, then paused at a smaller, open air casino. "Okay. That plump woman there, at the nickel slots."

"Absolutely not. She'd smother you in rich cooking."

"Wait. That's a liability?"

"You're a meat and potatoes man."

The oddest expression crossed Burke's face, as if he knew she was right, but couldn't bring himself to admit it. "The one carrying the dog?" he pressed. "Over there."

The well-groomed Pekingese sported a jeweled collar,

two pink bows and a doggie coat. "Wrong priorities. You'd be in competition with her pet."

"The one in the black, in the doorway."

The "black" Burke referred to was all Lycra, low in front and slit up to the thigh. "Attention seeker," she said dismissively. "Forget it."

"Okay, okay," he muttered, as a thread of desperation crept into his voice, "that one. In ruffles and lace."

Cupid paused. Now this woman was kind looking, pleasant. She certainly appeared honest. But it was the full skirt, and the blouse with the Peter Pan collar buttoned up to her neck, that disturbed Cupid. "Nope. Too prim."

"Arrghh!" he choked out. "You introduce two complete strangers in a casino, and they fall all over themselves. Why, I could practically see the stars in their eyes! If you can do that for someone else, why can't you do it for me?"

"It's going to happen, Burke. All in good time."

"But we're running out of time, Cupid. We've only got two days left. That's one day to find her and one day to marry her off to me."

# Chapter Ten

Burke's words haunted Cupid. She didn't know why she couldn't find a match for him. She just couldn't. She had spent the entire second day of their trip evaluating women. Every time she saw a woman she thought might do, it was as if she intentionally found something wrong with her.

Maybe Cupid just didn't want to give him away. She had never enjoyed a man's company so much in her entire life. She kept finding all these things out about him that she appreciated, and they were toppling her resolve. There were moments when she didn't know if she could bear to part with him, to be alone again.

Yet she'd promised him that she'd find him a wife. She intended to find him a mate. She intended to make him happy...but it was all becoming a conundrum. She wanted to make him happier than anyone had ever been before. She wanted to break the glass ceiling.

She wanted to find him a love that would be so enthralling, so committed and absolute that it would be painful. Downright painful. There was something in her that wanted the man to physically ache with a love he had to recognize and acknowledge.

The thing that was messing up her radar, as well as her instincts, was that she was attracted to him. That had never happened before. She'd never, ever, been attracted to a client. She'd gone out and done her job, then happily washed her hands of the whole affair.

Burke was different. He left her feeling torn and unfulfilled. It was inconceivable to admit he was driving her to distraction—but it was true. It was as if a madness had overtaken her, and she felt helpless to stop it. It kept growing and growing, until sometimes she felt as if she couldn't get enough of the man. She couldn't imagine how she was ever going to let him go. Especially not to another. To see him with another woman, to watch him smile at her, to put his arm around her shoulders or touch her hair, would be unbearable.

It was not out of the question to make a match with him herself. It had been done. However, past history on the issue was split. There had been some dreadful outcomes, and Cupid wasn't sure she could bring herself to risk those consequences.

Her aunt Sirena had given herself to a man under false pretenses, and lost all her powers. While they led a complacent life, her aunt had always pined for her lost gift.

If Cupid gave herself with a love that was not returned, she could lose the biggest part of herself, intrinsic in her being—to bring other people love and happiness.

Burke had warned her he didn't believe in love. He wanted a woman to share his life with, but didn't feel the obligation to love her.

That statement was an aggravation, a dilemma. She

knew she could make him love—to some degree—a mere mortal. But love herself? Would their silent resolutions, to love or not to love, create an unwitting power struggle between them?

Burke had a strength of conviction that was baffling. She couldn't fathom it. She had never met a man who was so self-assured, who possessed such a dogged willpower. In his own way, his strength matched hers. A lesser man she could conquer. But Burke? He had indomitable spirit and resolve.

She didn't know what her chances would be, should there be a union between them.

He would be good and kind. He'd be fair. But would he ever truly give his heart away?

In him, Cupid saw an Adonis, one who could strip her of her powers. She simply could not risk deception, not in this matter. Why, Burke's sheer will could be too much for her to overcome, and although she was exceedingly good, Cupid had doubts about the strength of her gift—especially when it came up against the formidable drive of Burke Riley.

No. It would be best to make him a match. To wash her hands of the matter and let him have his own life. What he chose to do with it, how he chose to love, would be his decision.

The hazards were too great.

That night, during dinner, she would make a match for him. She had no other choice.


"Are you sure you don't mind eating at the hotel again?" Burke asked, offering her the basket of hot, homemade bread.

"This hotel has five restaurants," she said, taking a slice from the loaf and laying it on the edge of her salad bowl. "It doesn't even feel like we're at the same place."

Burke grinned and pasted a hefty wedge of butter on his bread. "Kind of miss that violinist, though. That was a nice touch."

Cupid offered a conciliatory smile and forced her attention on the woman eating alone, two tables away. She guessed, by the way the woman had been scrutinizing the men in the restaurant, that she was another dental hygienist on the prowl. Or maybe, with the dental convention in town, Cupid would strike pay dirt and snag Burke a woman with a DDS after her name. That would be a kick. The rancher and the orthodontist.

The wry joke took the edge off her personal pain.

"Look," she said, "thanks for understanding about not having the photo retaken. I can't see that it would do much good, not if you're going to be trotting off into the sunset with someone else. And it just might make her jealous."

"Not a good way to start, I suppose."

"No." Cupid shot another glance at the woman. She was neat, well-dressed, but not flashy or ostentatious. She was well-mannered, and courteous to her server, even after he'd spilled wine on her skirt.

"Cupid?"

"Yes?"

"You seem distracted."

"Oh, I…was just thinking about how it will be when you're married."

"Oh."

"We'll probably never see each other again."

"You'll go your way, I'll go mine. Is that it?"

"I suppose. I'll just go back to being the postmistress at the Valentine post office, and you'll start having to think about things like anniversaries and new washing machines and whether she's allergic to your dog.''

He chuckled. "Laddie? How'd you know I have a dog?''

"Every ranch has a dog, doesn't it? Kind of like an outdoor doorbell. So, when you're in the barn, you know who's coming and going.''

"At least he's useful for something,'' Burke admitted. "You know, you'd like him.''

"Why's that?''

"He's got this heart-shaped patch of white just under his chin. I kind of figure you two would identify with each other.''

"Cute.'' Cupid experienced the strangest sense of loss, knowing she'd never know Laddie, never make friends with him, or have him lick her hands or whack his tail against her legs. "He's a big dog, isn't he?''

"What else? A shepherd mix. Yeah, we're two old castoffs that wound up together.''

Cupid winced. The man needed to be loved. He needed that, more than he realized. She had to put things in motion now, before she learned too much more about him, before she came to care too much.

She fingered the silver dollar in her pocket. Tonight she would gamble with it.

The woman, dressed in the most fetching blue, caught her eye and smiled.

*Do it,* Cupid told herself. *Do it now!*

The waiter bustled by, breaking her concentration.

Okay. Wait until after the entrée. A good meal would settle her queasy stomach. It would help her get through this debacle.

They placed the entrée in front of her too soon. She looked down at the seafood platter and the strangest thought went zinging through her head. This was like shooting fish in a barrel. She'd pluck some unlucky lady out of this restaurant and serve her up to Burke, whether he wanted her or not.

Cupid picked at her food and watched Burke plow through his. Every bit of small talk he tossed out drew her more firmly into his web. She struggled against the binding force, but it enveloped her with silky strands of need, of hope.

Drawing a deep, rasping breath, Cupid plunged her hand into her pocket and clutched the silver dollar. She silently repeated her mantra, knowing it alone would give her the strength to get through this.

*Smitten, with an arrow to the heart, lost forever to Cupid's dart.*

She dropped the coin, noisily, and willed it to roll beneath the woman's chair and strike her shoe.

The brunette shuffled her feet out of the way and peered over the side of her chair.

"Oh, I'm sorry, I guess I'm all thumbs today," Cupid apologized as the woman picked it up and offered it back. "Thank you."

"No problem," she said. "I knocked over my whole cup of quarters yesterday and everyone in the lounge ended up crawling all over the floor, helping me pick them up. Strange place, isn't it, where you carry a week's salary in a plastic cup."

"It is, yes. But it sounds like you're having a good time in Vegas," Cupid commented conversationally, dropping the silver dollar back in her pocket.

"Wonderful. I'm here for the dental convention."

Bingo. "It seems like everyone is," Cupid replied. "Where are you from?"

"Kansas City."

"Really? Well, at least we share the same home state." Cupid looked at Burke, to judge his response and draw him into the conversation.

He merely lounged against the back of his chair and, with the most patient smile on his face, waited for her to continue.

For a few moments Cupid and the woman exchanged pleasantries about living on opposite sides of the state. "So, are you here—" Cupid tensed, in anticipation of the question she hated to ask "—alone?"

"A couple of girls from my office are with me. Since we're all single, we travel together a lot."

"Oh." Cupid's reply was short, succinct and disappointed. Burke, drat him, didn't offer her one smidgen of help.

"They wanted to see a show tonight," the woman added, "but I said I'd stay in. I absolutely love the excitement of this place, but sometimes I have to take a breather. My folks always said I was more suited to the wide-open spaces."

Cupid couldn't have felt any worse if someone had driven a stake through her heart. She was right on the verge of giving Burke away—to someone who would be perfect for him. "I...I don't think I caught your name," she said breathlessly.

"Vivian. Vivian Bliss."

*Bliss?* As in *wedded bliss?* She should take it as a sign, she knew she should.

"Well, my name's Cupid Jones, and—"

"Cupid? Is that really your name?" Vivian smiled, obviously delighted.

"It is. I guess if there's a skier that can be named Picabo, there can be a postmistress named Cupid." Cupid paused and tried to control her hammering, yammering heart. "And, Vivian, this is…" *Do it.* Do it now! Say it and be done with it. Cupid doggedly plunged ahead. "This is…" For the life of her, she couldn't utter his name. It was as if she'd swallowed a cylinder of air and was holding her breath. The pain behind her breastbone became so horrific, she thought she'd die. "A…a friend of mine," she finished lamely, "from Kansas."

Burke said nothing, just nodded.

Before her eyes rolled back in her head—from the sheer idiocy of the introduction—Cupid glimpsed Burke's mouth curl in amusement. Still he said nothing, and picked the plastic wrap off a round toothpick, then jammed it between his lips, a signal he was done with the meal.

"It's nice to meet you," Vivian said graciously. "I thought, while I was eating, that you made such a lovely couple."

"Thank you. But I'm sorry, I didn't introduce you to—" both Burke and Vivian gazed at her expectantly "—to him, because…" This was Cupid's last shot. It was now or never.

Now, her rational mind urged.

Never, her subconscious railed.

She couldn't do it.

An ominous sense of failure and relief washed through Cupid. "Because I don't feel well. If you'll excuse me, please."

Cupid turned and fled from the table, unaware when Burke tipped his head to the well-dressed, soft-spoken woman. "Ma'am," he said, excusing himself, "I want to check on her."

Cupid slumped against the cool, mirror-covered wall next to the elevator and closed her eyes. She was drained, positively wiped out. She had just walked away from what had the potential to be the best possible match of her career. Her mother would have rejoiced. Lysandra would have been absolutely giddy.

But Cupid had bungled it. She had single-handedly turned one simple "Burke, this is Vivian... Vivian, this is Burke," into a fiasco.

Well, it was up to Burke now. Let him find his own bride. He could make his own introductions, she argued. After all, she'd given him an opening. All he had to do was take the opportunity and run with it.

*Burke, tell Miss Bliss that your friend Cupid is an airhead, and ignore her.*

The only thing Cupid wanted to do right now was crawl into that great big, heart-shaped bed and pull the covers over her head. Maybe the Fates would look down on her and give her a match for redemption. Maybe they'd feel sorry for how inept and incompetent she was.

If she ever got a second chance, she'd pounce on it.

"Going up? Fourteenth floor," a familiar voice beside her said.

Cupid's eyes flew open. She whirled and looked straight into Burke's smoky gaze. "You? I thought you—and she—would, you know...take up where I left off."

Burke shook his head. "Nah."

"Nah? What do you mean, 'nah'? She's perfect for you! Get back in there and marry her! Burke, don't lose her now," she chided. "It took me all day to find her!"

"She wasn't my type."

Cupid stared at him, openmouthed. "Not your type? Have you lost your mind?"

Burke pensively studied her, his expression going

dark. "Possibly. Now, I'm holding the elevator. And I've told the concierge we'll take that midnight massage. Tonight. I think you need it."

They rode up to their room in silence. Burke slid the card key into the door and, with the green light flashing, Cupid put a hand on his sleeve, stopping him. "I thought you wanted to go out tonight."

"We've had a full day. I'm satisfied."

"I feel like I'm holding you back. So if you want to go out, and don't want me to be here when you get back, I'd understand. I can make other arrangements."

"I want you to be here when I get back, Cupid."

A shuddery feeling shot through her chest. If she didn't know better, she would have thought she'd been struck by her own love-tipped arrow.

Burke ushered her inside. The room had been made up and a huge fruit basket, with chocolate-dipped strawberries and sugar-glazed orange slices, was arranged on the marble-topped table. An attached card read, "Best wishes to the happy couple, from the Management."

Cupid stared at it. "Burke, we need to talk." She turned to him imploringly. "Everyone thinks we're married, or getting married—and I should have introduced you to that woman down there, but I couldn't bring myself to do it."

"I know."

"You…know?"

He chuckled. "Yes…but I rather enjoyed watching you find something wrong with every woman out there. I was waiting to find out what was wrong with her."

"Don't you get it? I couldn't find anything! She was perfect."

"I kind of figured that."

"Then why…?"

"Why didn't I do something about it?" he inquired. "Because I looked at her...and I looked at you...and I figured I'd rather be with you."

Cupid stopped, her mind reeling. "You did?"

"Yep. Not a doubt in my mind."

"But I thought you wanted to get married." Cupid stared at him in confusion. "I suppose if I knew, really, *why* you wanted to get married it would help, but—"

"Very simple," he said gently. "It's true that I have a nice life, and I'd like to share it, just as I said. But there's more, I guess. I'd like a child, someone to inherit my place, someone to remember me—in a good way," he qualified. "Kind of like leaving my mark on the world, and saying I didn't leave it in such a bad way, or leave an unfinished, empty life behind me. I don't want to live my old man's life, don't want to be remembered that way. I'd kind of like to change things a little bit."

It was an eloquent speech, especially for a man from the western plains of Kansas, one who wanted to be known as a rancher, not a cowboy. One who professed that solitude eased a man's soul, while chaos jangled his best intentions. Cupid was moved, visibly, though she choked back the emotion.

She instinctively stepped into his arms to offer a comforting hug. It became an embrace, then a melding of two hungry souls. He nuzzled her cheek, brushed a feather-light kiss against her ear, her temple.

"Those are admirable, valid reasons," she whispered. "All of them."

He wrapped his arms around her, pulling her tighter. "So glad you approve," he said, his voice going husky.

"You didn't do your research, though."

He lifted his head. "What? How's that?"

"Because if you wanted to have a family…well, Moira couldn't have children. She told me."

A flicker of surprise put his jaw off center. "I just assumed."

"Most men would, I guess."

He grew silent for a moment. "I wouldn't have faulted her for it. I want you to know that." A shred of trepidation burrowed into Cupid's consciousness. Did he have regrets? "But maybe things worked out for the best. I heard she already married that hardware guy and has his three little girls wrapped around her finger."

"She was meant to be a mom," Cupid agreed, grateful when Burke's arm tightened about her a second time. "Men think of heirs and women think of children. I always wanted to be a mom. I just love babies. There's something about their innocence, their trust—" Cupid broke off, aware of her momentary lapse of judgment. She seemed to have too many of them these days, especially around Burke.

"You ever wonder," he said, "if things were supposed to work out this way?"

Cupid faltered. He couldn't guess how many times. "It's occurred to me," she said carefully.

"Marry me, Cupid," he proposed. "Be the wife, the mate, you promised me."

Grappling with all her internal feelings, Cupid slid her hands over his shoulders, her fingers inching under his collar, then curling around his lapels. "That would change everything," she warned.

He looked at her, not comprehending her meaning. "The chapel is still booked for 11:00 a.m. tomorrow morning. We could both have what we want. No surrogate-mother stuff for me, no out-of-wedlock babies, mail-order brides or arranged marriages. Everything legitimate. Right from the get-go.''

A quickie marriage was never what Cupid had envisioned. She'd imagined a long, passionate courtship, a flowery wedding, with organza and lace and yards and yards of white tulle. It didn't matter so much that this would be a private affair, without friends or family, because her family believed in the longstanding value of the institution of marriage. The ceremony was only the briefest part of it, and specifically for two people. But it was the tacky commercialism she rebelled against. She didn't want a rented gown, and a bouquet of flowers with a gold foil sticker lost in the depths of them that said Made in Japan.

"Tomorrow's Valentine's Day," Burke reminded her. "It's also your birthday. How about instead of a cake and candles, I give you a marriage certificate? And a wedding to go with it?"

She knew Burke was teasing her, waiting for her answer, yet her mind raced ahead, working like a spreadsheet and balancing all the signs, the directions they should take. The significance of the dates, Burke's contact with her birthmark, his seeming acceptance of her matchmaking powers, the defection of his mail-order bride, and even Cupid's own unruly feelings—it all added up to a deeper meaning.

Perhaps, she reasoned, fate had intervened, causing this upheaval, this interruption in the flow of her life. She could refuse, but no one she knew had ever turned his or her back on the Fates before.

It could be foolhardy for her to do something like that now.

Take the plunge, a little voice inside her head urged.
Take the plunge and forget the risks!

"I think, Burke," she said bravely, "that you've just
found yourself a wife."

## *Chapter Eleven*

Burke stared at Cupid, momentarily stunned. He hadn't really expected her to accept his proposal.

She was everything beautiful and good, and he guessed instinctively that she could have anyone she wanted. Yet she'd said she would marry him. He'd even told her, in flat-out terms, that he didn't believe in love; she surely knew that that would never change, and still she'd accepted it.

An expectant moment passed between them. He was filled with a crazy mixture of awe and surprise, which for the briefest of moments almost incapacitated him.

He knew he should take her in his arms. Kiss her. Hold her. Make plans for tomorrow, for a lifetime.

Yet he couldn't seem to move. Odd, how easy it had been last night, or even moments ago, when they needed to comfort each other, or had lain in each other's arms, talking and reminiscing. He wanted that acceptance—that bond—between them for a lifetime.

Realizing that, he chose his first words as a promised

man carefully, choosing not to delude Cupid with false words or promises.

"I know we can be happy together," he said, his gaze lighting on her lips, his arm reaching for her. She came to him of her own volition, and he hugged her close, then pressed a kiss against her forehead, her temple. "I'll do my best to make sure you don't have any regrets."

"Let's not talk about regrets," she said softly, her breath warm against his chin, his cheek. "Not yet. Sometimes, I think this was meant to be."

He laughed, believing she had truly accepted what their life would be like. A partnership, with an agreement they'd both honor. "Then we can seal this deal with a kiss?" he prompted.

"Mmm." She turned her face up for his kiss, his touch.

He regarded her, struck by how much he had gained in such a short, remarkable time. This vexing, determined woman made his head clear, and put a new purpose before him. She made his blood grow hot and his imagination run rampant.

She was good for him; he had no doubt about that.

Planting his thumb on her chin, he tipped her head up for his kiss. Intentionally prolonging the moment, he let it fill with expectation, anticipation. Then his head dropped to her level and he claimed her, opening her mouth between his questing lips, his tongue darting in and out to taste, and savor, all her sweetness.

They swayed for a moment, both silently knowing they would soon be bound together as man and woman, husband and wife. They would belong to each other.

The kiss ended, yet they clung together.

"Tell me. Is it true this town never sleeps?" Cupid asked shakily, against his shoulder.

He chuckled. "I should hope not. For I do have plans to sleep with my new wife." Cupid ducked her head, a sudden, inviting blush invading her cheeks. "Why? Why do you want to know?"

"Because I'd hoped to get a wedding dress, and real flowers. And there's so little time."

"Tomorrow morning. First thing. You can pick something out in the bridal shop downstairs and have it sent to the chapel. Or—"

"No. I'd like you to go with me. To pick it out."

He paused. "I thought it was bad luck for the bride to be seen in her wedding gown."

"I don't believe in any of that superstitious stuff," she scoffed. "I don't believe any of that malarkey. None of that 'something old, something blue' stuff. It's all made up and hokey. Marriage isn't any of those things, it's what we bring to it."

Hearing the hope in her voice, Burke narrowed his gaze. Damn, he didn't want to disappoint her. He'd be fair and honest, but she had to know up front what she was getting: a hardworking man who had bargained his way into a traditional family. That was all. Emotional attachments were nice for those who could afford them; for most folks, they were a liability.

It was just that he cared for her so damn much that he didn't want to disappoint her.

A knock sounded at the door, startling them, and both Burke and Cupid pulled apart guiltily. The intimate mood was broken, and so were his intentions to set things straight.

Burke strode to the door, somewhat annoyed by the intrusion. "Yes?"

"We're here for your midnight massage, sir." A professional looking couple in their late twenties swept into the room, each carrying a folding table. "It will only take a few minutes for setup, but you're scheduled for an hour's massage."

"I have drapes for you both." The woman smiled, handing them each a warmed sheet. "You can take off everything above the waist, and anything that's uncomfortable below the waist." She nodded toward the bathroom. "The wrap goes around your back, under your arms, and lap it over in front. Come out when you're ready."

Burke cast an apprehensive glance at Cupid's frozen expression. Maybe this wasn't such a good idea. Not now.

"My name's Sandy, and both Jim and I are nationally certified massage therapists," the woman continued, oblivious to Cupid's reaction. "We specialize in Swedish massage and relaxation therapy, and tonight we'll target the neck, shoulders and back. High stress areas. I can almost guarantee that in less than an hour you'll feel one hundred percent better about everything."

Jim switched on the portable CD player and soft, classical music filled the room.

"Cupid?" Burke inquired solicitously. "Do you want to go ahead with it?"

She dragged her eyes away from the oils and lotions Jim was methodically arranging on a nearby table. "Yes," she said, clutching the sheet to her chest, "to everything, including the massage."

In fifteen minutes they were both stretched out on collapsible massage tables, discreetly covered by identical peach-colored sheets. The lights had been dimmed to a dull glow and Jim had turned on the gas fireplace. For ambience, he said.

Sandy asked if they objected to scents, or an aromatherapy treatment, and when they said they didn't, promptly put simmering crystals in a potpourri pot to warm. Tranquility, she announced.

Burke, who had never once been pampered in all of his rancher's life, let Jim pummel and knead and rearrange his work-worn muscles. He breathed in the scent called tranquillity, while the comforting melody of some unknown pianist lulled his mind. The room was warm and drugged his senses. The massage oil seeping into his body was slick and hot.

Beside him, Cupid was on her stomach, her drape artfully arranged to cover her hips and cascade onto the table in a rumpled puddle. Feasting his gaze upon the curve of her spine, the flattened globes of her breasts, Burke felt his fascination grow.

He'd seen a woman's bare back before. He'd certainly seen more of a woman's breasts than he was glimpsing now. Yet he'd never experienced a more provocative, more reverent moment than this in his entire lifetime.

He knew now why artists and sculptors studied a woman's body, were fascinated with it, tried to duplicate it. There was something so mysterious, so inviting, so alluring, that it captivated a man, making him go weak and hungry. Making him desire something—an essence, perhaps—that he couldn't define.

Cupid was the woman artists strove to replicate on canvas and in stone.

Her strawberry-gold hair was all atumble, curling onto her nape like that of a Greek goddess. The arching column of her neck reminded him of statues he had seen in museums. She was perfection, her flesh as sleek and shiny as alabaster. The massage oil gave her a burnished, opalescent look.

It was almost inconceivable that she would live with him on the ranch, share his life, bear his children. The realization filled him with trepidation, awe. Perhaps this was a bigger undertaking than he had estimated when he offered the proposal.

"I'm going to dust you with a little body talc, if that's all right, sir," Jim said, moving to the tray of lotions and potions and creams, "to absorb the oil."

Burke grunted wordlessly in acknowledgment.

Over his head, he could feel Jim smiling. "Never had a massage before, huh?" he observed. "Takes a little something out of you the first time."

Cupid stretched, languishing on the table, as Sandy peppered her with powder, then paused to dust her with a silky, fat brush. "Wonderful," she breathed.

Burke, acutely conscious of the rise and fall of her chest, was full of emotion, alive with sensuality. He wanted to hold her, but his arms felt ridiculously weak and heavy.

"We'll start cleaning up," Sandy said softly, drawing the sheet up over Cupid's back, her sides. "Take your time sitting up. You may be a little bit dizzy at first."

Both Burke and Cupid sat on the edge of the tables, their feet dangling. They smiled at each other drunkenly, sated with an uncommon headiness, and pleasure. Burke stood first, knotting the sheet around his middle.

Cupid slid off the table and crossed her arms over her chest, pinning the drape in place.

The music faded, until only the low snapping sound of the gas fireplace filled the heated room. The massage therapists worked quickly, putting away their wares, their amazingly torturous tools of deception and delight.

"No need to change," Sandy instructed quietly. "You can leave the sheets and towels for the hotel staff."

Burke offered them a hefty tip and saw them to the door.

He turned back to Cupid. She stood in the middle of the room, the firelight putting a reddish tinge to her tousled hair. The sheet bunched about her middle, exposing her bare shoulders and pooling at her feet.

"That was decadent," she declared.

"And aren't you glad I remembered to arrange it?"

She offered up a Mona Lisa–like smile. "It makes me think you have some potential as a husband. I'll change, and we can…" Her attention drifted over to the heart-shaped bed.

"Changing isn't necessary," he said huskily. "If you don't want to."

Her brow suddenly furrowed, as if she were torn. "But it is. For me. We aren't married yet."

His arms hung uselessly at his sides, when all he wanted to do was hold her, discover her. "We will be."

"I may not believe in old wives' tales, or superstitions or myths…but I do believe there is a right order to things, Burke."

"I understand." He didn't. Not at all. It was all foreign to the way he'd been raised. In his experience, men did what they wanted, and women put up with what they could, and hightailed it out after they'd had their fill. But he'd vowed to realign his life and reshape his outlook. Perhaps this was part of it. The making concessions, the awareness of someone else. "Will you want to call your folks? Let them know you're—we're—getting married?"

She shook her head and moved in the direction of the bath. "That's not necessary." She paused, her hand on the gold door handle. "They know I'll make the right choices…and follow my heart."

Cupid hastily changed, not wanting to be away from Burke for even seconds. Yet sleeping with him, after all that had transpired, was awkward.

Without even knowing it, she had put away the last of her single life. She would never again sleep alone, in her double bed, in Valentine. She had changed. Now there was not just one of her, but two. Two pillows on a bed. One blanket to share.

Cupid knew, without him asking, that she would follow him to his ranch outside Thurlby. Her life would never again be the same. She accepted that without regrets. It simply startled her, how quickly she knew what she wanted. She wanted Burke. She wanted to blend their lives and create something good, and new, and whole.

In bed, together, he offered her his arm again, and she made use of it. They stared drowsily at the ceiling and talked, just as they had the night before. But this time everything was different. They were together—and they were apart. Cupid wondered idly what tomorrow night, their next night in this bed, would bring.

"A good-night kiss," Burke finally ventured, his voice husky.

Cupid turned in his arms and offered up that deepest part of herself. She lost herself to his mouth, to the weight of his body atop hers. When his hand strayed to her waist, her ribs, she moved beneath him, accompanying him.

He covered her breast, stroking her flesh inquisitively through the folds of her nightgown. Almost immediately, burgeoning heat and passion transported her and the intensity of her desires escalated, rendering her powerless to his advances.

Yet his caresses ceased, even as Cupid arched, involuntarily wanting more. "Burke...?"

"No," he whispered, almost as if he were talking to himself. "Tonight I'll offer you reason and good sense, but tomorrow I'll offer you the passions that bond a man and woman."

When he drew back from her, groaning, she knew how much he wanted her. She recognized the tightly reined control he kept over himself.

They held each other for some moments, and then she drifted off, mentally preparing a to-do list for tomorrow, her wedding day. Doing so took her mind off the possibility that Burke might never say he loved her.


Cupid swept out of the dressing room and into the exquisite showroom.

The strangest expression crossed the saleslady's features. "Why, isn't that odd? I didn't realize that gown came in blush."

Cupid knew full well that it wasn't the gown at all, but the pinkish haze that clung to her during those rare moments of emotional upheaval. "It's probably my coloring," she said. "Redheads cast a long shadow."

"Either way, it's positively stunning on you," the woman gushed. She turned to Burke. "What do you think?"

Burke nodded appreciatively, his gaze lingering on the off-the-shoulder neckline. The long, tight sleeves were appliquéd with bits of trailing ivy, while the bodice, entirely appliquéd, came to a point in the front before jetting into a full skirt of organza. Burke's inspection drifted down to the hem, which was trimmed in two narrow bands of satin.

"Do you like it?" Cupid persisted. "Or—"

"No, it's fine."

"It might be a little overdone—" she lowered her voice "—for the two of us." The saleswoman discreetly removed herself from what she sensed was a private conversation. "But I want to have something we'll both remember," Cupid said softly. "So when you recall our wedding day, you'll always think of me like this."

A faint smile curved his lips, and he rocked back on his heels, considering. "Remembering you like this...it's not a half-bad memory."

"I've no need for a veil. I'll just—"

"Yes," he said quickly. "You do."

"I have a lovely illusion veil," the sales woman interjected. "It would enhance the gown. If you'd like to see it...?"

"We would," Burke said decisively.

Cupid was immediately fitted with a veil. Made of seed pearls and tiny opalescent hearts, it circled the back of her head like a halo.

"Appropriate," Burke said approvingly, "since the girl's partial to hearts."

"Really?" The saleswoman brightened. "Then I have the perfect pair of slippers." She scurried to the back room and brought out a small pair of white kidskin slippers, the toe of which was inset with a satin heart outlined in tiny seed pearls.

"Oh, my..." Cupid automatically reached for them.

"They're the last pair," the saleslady warned, "and we're not getting any more in."

Cupid's hand fell back, and she willed herself to resist. Besides, they might not fit. "Of course, I thought I could just wear my sandals. They're practical, they're paid for. They make sense."

Burke took the shoe from the saleswoman. "Let me," he offered, indicating Cupid should try them on.

She backed into the chair the saleswoman offered. Her frothy gown mounded over her lap and spilled onto the floor. Picking up her hem, she lifted the gown to her knees and extended one silk-stockinged foot.

Burke sank to one knee in one sensuous move. He cupped the back of her calf, then slid his palm down to her heel, to guide her foot into the slipper. "It fits," he declared.

Cupid wiggled her foot, turning it so the heart-shaped insert would catch and reflect the light. "And it makes me feel a bit like Cinderella."

His mouth quirked. "That's okay, then, because I didn't get down on my knee to propose." Behind them, they heard the saleswoman sniff with disdain, that he would even admit to such a thing. Burke and Cupid exchanged small, tentative smiles.

"No," Cupid said, "I meant, to think that I have found my prince."

Burke's brow imperceptibly furrowed, and his gaze went dark, unreadable, as he looked up and over Cupid's head. "We'll take it all," he said to the saleswoman, "and she better just wear it, otherwise we'll be late for our own wedding."

# Chapter Twelve

The wedding chapel was little more than a niche carved out of a humongous twenty-story hotel and casino empire.

"And we have one 'wedding to go'," the elderly receptionist behind the counter chirped. "This is your basic economy plan, but definitely your best value." She reached under the counter and pulled out a frazzled looking bouquet. She handed it to Cupid. "For the complimentary eight by ten. You may hold it during the ceremony if you wish."

"It's plastic."

"I know. But it doesn't show in the pictures."

Most of the flowers were unidentifiable, the rest looked like they had been sat on by the bride of Frankenstein. "It's fake," Cupid enunciated, this time a little louder.

The woman's thin mouth pursed. "Perhaps you'd like a single stem," she suggested, looking at the clock. She flopped a long-stemmed, red silk rose on the counter.

Flower-on-a-stick, Cupid thought. The stem looked like it was cut from a green wire hanger; the petals were ragged and wilted looking.

"Pick one," the woman instructed. "We're on a tight schedule. Today's Valentine's Day. Biggest day of the year."

"And don't I know it," Cupid muttered, casting a surreptitious glance at Burke, who was at another counter, paying for the wedding package. He turned, as if he could feel her eyes boring into him.

"Everything okay?" he mouthed.

Cupid shook her head. "I can't handle this." She lifted the bedraggled bouquet with one hand and pointed the wilted rose at him like it was a wand. "They call these things flowers."

"They look perfectly nice in the pictures, dear," the woman intoned. "They're only for effect. No one needs to know."

"But *I* know," Cupid wailed. "It'll mess up the direction, change the aura."

Burke lifted a finger to stop her tirade, then signed the credit card voucher with one hand. "Wait. It's okay." He came to Cupid's side and handed the plastic blossoms back to the receptionist. "I ordered flowers this morning. Haven't they arrived?"

The receptionist frowned. "Well…we did get these. But I thought they were a joke, from the hotel flower shop." She pulled out a large, beribboned box and tapped the card. "See?"

It was addressed to Cupid. Simply Cupid.

"That's me," Cupid said evenly. "I'm Cupid."

The woman tittered, but tried not to laugh. "Clever," she finally muttered. "You gettin' married on Valentine's Day."

"I didn't plan it that way," Cupid said, distracted, as she slipped the ribbon from the box.

"But I did," Burke volunteered.

"Yes," Cupid reminded him, "but that was when you were going to marry that other woman." She traced one of the red sweetheart roses in the cascading bridal bouquet, and noticed the receptionist's eyebrows arch above her bifocals. "Thank you," Cupid said to Burke, "for remembering."

The doors to the chapel opened and a happy couple exited. The receptionist reflexively reached into a bag of confetti and flung a little at their heads, while the timed-release camera snapped a picture for future generations. "You're next," she said. "Let me start the music, and you can take your places."

Cupid adjusted her bouquet and peered between the open chapel doors. A rotund justice of the peace, with his black book opened in his hands, waited impatiently at the end of a very short aisle. If a bride was a deep thinker, there would hardly be time, as she walked down the aisle, to change her mind and back out.

Burke walked ahead of Cupid and stood beside the justice of the peace.

"This is not what I expected," Cupid said to no one in particular, not to the receptionist, or the two paid witnesses who sat, looking bored, in the back of the church. "Not in my wildest."

"This is Valentine's Day," the receptionist reminded her. "We move 'em out, we move 'em in. Keep in mind, honey, it's the thought that counts."

With that, Cupid set her eyes on Burke and moved forward, down the aisle and to her destiny. She loved him, she knew she did. Otherwise this would all be for naught.

While one could never really know what was in another's heart, Cupid believed Burke loved her—either
that or she could make him love her. That would be the
only way, really, for her to resolve her past and come
into her future.

Burke would be the bridge to the rest of her life, and
her happiness depended on it. Perhaps now he could not
admit his feelings, but he had affection for her, she was
sure. She saw it in his face, in everything he did for her.

It took less than a dozen small steps to join him, but
just as many doubts crowded her mind. The ceremony
was bare-bones traditional. Yet when Burke said "I do,"
Cupid looked deep into his eyes and was certain she
glimpsed the depths of his soul.

It was pure and tender, and though she saw the
bruises, it gave her hope.

"You may kiss the bride!" the justice of the peace
announced. He stepped on a foot pedal and strains of
the wedding march crashed over the loudspeakers, indicating the ceremony had concluded and they were to
make their way back into the bride and groom holding
tank.

They endured the whap in the face with the confetti,
posed for several more expensive pictures, then were
freed to the streets of Las Vegas.

They paused beneath a flashing neon sign that adver-
tised Loose Slots, while the atmosphere between them
seemed more like "loose ends." Burke hunched against
the desert wind, and Cupid's gown and veil swirled
about her.

Finally, he reached for her hand and tucked it into his
pocket. They walked to the street corner before he
paused. "You ever want to kiss someone on a street

corner, in the middle of everyone and everything, just because you can? Just because you're married?"

Cupid's mouth lifted at the corners. "I've never been married before," she confided, a coquettish tilt to her head.

"Me neither." He lowered his face to hers, pulling her into a tight, possessive embrace. He offered up a sweet seductive kiss, then trailed a hot path of kisses down her throat and onto her bare shoulder.

Behind them, cars honked. Men whistled and teenage girls giggled.

He reluctantly pulled back, oblivious to the attention they drew. "I've made reservations for lunch, and then…whatever."

The implication was clear. Cupid knew what "whatever" meant, and it made her shiver with anticipation.

It was dusk when they returned to their hotel room. There were times during the day when Cupid suspected Burke had dreamed up excuses to avoid going back to the hotel. In their wedding duds they had wandered through casinos, shopped and accepted strangers' congratulations.

At one point, Cupid put the twenty dollars her father had sent with her on number 14, figuring the conditions, the events and the timing was right. To her surprise, they didn't win a thing. She brushed it off and refused to take it as a sign.

Just before dusk, they returned to their room.

"Did you want to call your folks and tell them the news?" Burke asked, loosening his tie. "Tell your dad you lost all his money?"

She laughed and shook her head, carefully laying her bouquet on a side table. "We can tell them together when we get home. It'll be best for them to meet you first.'' She paused, watching Burke shrug out of his jacket. It suddenly hit her that he was her husband. ''They're going to like you, you know.''

He stopped, as if her praise was quite unexpected, then hung his coat over the back of a chair. ''For marrying their little girl, with no advance notice, no fair warning?''

''My parents want me to be happy, and they've always trusted my choices. They'd trust me to do the right thing, especially where you and a wedding was concerned.''

Glancing out the window, as if he were suddenly uncomfortable, Burke headed for the bottle of champagne. He pulled it out of the bucket, oblivious to the spatters of water that darkened his pants. ''Hey. We've finally got a real reason to open another bottle now,'' he suggested, tipping it in her direction.

''Have you noticed there's *always* champagne on ice here?''

''Part of the bridal package, I guess.''

Cupid went behind the bar to get two flutes, while Burke wrapped a towel around the neck of the bottle and pulled the cork. ''Huh,'' he mused. ''Pink champagne.'' She stood beside him as he poured some into each of the glasses. ''I keep thinking I'm seeing you in all these rosy-colored hues.''

''You probably are.'' Her voice went low, and seductive as honey. She initiated a companionable clink of their glasses. ''I'm going to fit right into that pink kitchen of yours.''

A bemused expression touched his features. ''Life is strange, isn't it? I expected to wind up with a common wife, a run-of-the-mill woman who would meet my needs and be content with her lot. And then I got you."

Sensing a crack in his demeanor, Cupid pressed her advantage. "And what's that supposed to mean?"

"It means...that I never imagined you."

Cupid's nerved endings buzzed. It was a backhanded compliment, but it was the closest Burke had come to admitting any feelings at all. "Are you trying to say you've been 'Cupidized?'"

He snorted and drained his champagne flute, setting it on the bar. "More like *terrorized* by all this hearts and flowers stuff."

Cupid's resolve hardened, even as she grinned. Soon it would be her will against his.

She had grown up welcoming love; he had grown up resisting it. Did she have the perseverance to earn his trust? Could she tear down the walls he'd built around his heart? There was so little time, really.

The one thing she couldn't do was use her powers on him. Her love had to flow from her heart to his, and be reciprocated, for validation.

She sipped the champagne, then he slipped the flute from her hand, and set it beside his. "I want to kiss you," he said.

She voluntarily moved into his arms and lifted her head. *Love me, love me,* she implored silently.

He kissed her. Soundly. Until she was breathless. Until she lost rational thought.

He rasped the edge of his teeth against her jaw, then nibbled the pulse point in her neck. His tongue laved the spot, pumping liquid fire through her veins.

Cupid unwittingly writhed, to get closer, to fit her body against his. She rationally knew that she had to make him love her now, before this seduction went much further. But beneath his expert hands, her senses grew fuzzy with need, her thinking became unclear.

He put his palm on her breast, and she gasped. He chafed the peak, and she went taut.

Pressing a kiss against the top of her breast, Burke carefully avoided her sweet spot. "I married Cupid, on Valentine's Day," he said thickly against her flesh. "On her birthday. Is that poetic justice or what?"

"Poetic justice?" She leaned back against his supporting arm, vaguely aware he was working the buttons of her gown. "For what?"

Before he could answer, the bodice slipped off her shoulders, buckling forward. Her strapless bra, lacy and sheer, was held by a single clasp in the front, and Burke's fingers slipped between her breasts to release it. The elastic snapped, going limp. He nuzzled the garment away and mouthed her breasts. Cupid heard herself moan, instinctively moving so he could lap the sensitive peak of her breast. "For a man who doesn't believe in love," he mumbled hoarsely against her flesh, "it's all turned out to be a strange and puzzling contradiction."

Cupid sagged heavily against him, aching to believe Burke's ambiguous reply held a deeper, unrecognized, meaning. "Love," she whispered, "is a lot of things to a lot of people."

Burke chuckled throatily and bent to pick her up, snagging her beneath the knees in a flurry of skirts and rumpled organza.

He carried her to the heart-shaped bed and laid her atop the silken comforter as if he revered her, worshiped her. She pointed her toes and let him peel away her slippers. She lifted her hips to let him snare the voluminous gown and remove it. Her strapless bra had fallen away, leaving her bare-breasted, in only sheer white panties and thigh-high stockings.

He made an appreciative sound in the back of his throat and, putting his hand on the sensitive flesh between her thighs, hooked a finger under the top of one stocking and pulled it down. He did the same with the other.

With his eyes fixed on the tiny scrap of silk left to her, Burke shed his shirt and kicked his way out of his pants.

He was hard and huge and glistening when he tossed aside his briefs.

Cupid caught her breath and let her eyes drift closed, imagining their eventual coupling. His knee sank onto the mattress beside her, then he stretched out full-length, his fingers splaying over her waist, her rib cage, as he captured her and pulled her to him.

His chest rubbed against her breasts; his hips rode against her soft belly. His flesh was warm. There was strength in his hands; his arms and legs were peppered with coarse hair. When his chin grazed her shoulder, she felt the rasp of stubble and shivered.

So many sensations. All of them assaulting her, inviting her. Her mind was in a whirl. She loved this man, desperately. This was so right, all of it.

He rolled on his side, and she found herself lying partially beneath him.

"This will be the beginning of something good, sweet thing," he whispered, slipping his hand beneath the elastic holding the white silk. "The first time for us."

Cupid's response was gutteral, needy.

His hand slipped lower, to cover her mound and stroke. His forefinger found her cleft, and the softest, most sensitive bit of her flesh.

Cupid arched, her hips lifting, her shoulders straining against the mattress, her head going back.

When her convulsing body slowed, he delved deeper, to discover moist folds. With expert fingers, he caressed her, intentionally avoiding the tender area that begged for release.

She writhed, pressing nearer. "Burke...?"

"Wait," he whispered raggedly. "A bit longer...only a bit..." Rolling atop her, he swiped at her breasts with his mouth, then paused at a nipple to suckle.

Love words tore from her throat in a jumble; Burke merely chuckled, his hands kneading her softness to submission. His hand moved away, to inch her panties down and free her.

He probed with his manhood, inciting a dozen scintillating sparks to explode behind her eyelids.

"This is going to be our first memorable ride together," he said softly, burrowing between her legs.

There was something coarse, disturbing, about his pronouncement. Yet it was provocatively intimate, the way he teased. Her hands drifted up, to hug his shoulder blades, to pull him against her.

He nuzzled closer, sliding against her flesh. He purposely wet the head of his shaft with her fluids. When he tormented her with tiny, ineffective jabs, her legs went weak, falling farther and farther apart.

Burke settled in. His palms spanned her rib cage, his fingertips at the sides of her breasts. His hips lifted, poised momentarily, before he plunged into her soft wetness.

Cupid cried out. The pain was blinding, raw, and she clung to him.

Burke's eyes widened in surprise; his face contorted

with disbelief. He didn't move, staying rigidly imbedded in her.

"You—" The single utterance made him sway.

Cupid tensed at the movement and emitted a small gasp.

"Dammit," he growled, "if I'd known. That you'd never—" He clamped his jaws together and propped himself on his elbows.

"It's okay, it's okay," Cupid soothed. "It's... supposed to happen like that on your wedding night, isn't it?"

He groaned, the muscles in his shoulders bunching as he supported himself. "It's sure as hell supposed to be easier than this. When you know," he added gruffly. "I could have made it easier. The first time."

"I didn't know how to tell you. I thought maybe you'd guess."

He put his temple against hers. "I just don't want to hurt you," he said. "And it's going to take a little more hurt to get us there."

"It's okay."

Tunneling his arms between her back and the mattress, he cradled her, gently lifting. He started rocking, slowly, carefully. Her eyes closed. "It's gonna be better than this, I promise. I swear it."

Her smile was faint, and she endured the first tentative thrusts, surrendering to his ministrations.

Rocking and stroking, he moved inside her. He carved away at her virginity ever so slowly.

Looping her arms around him, she felt the pain ebb, igniting and fueling itself into ecstasy. Her body relaxed, melding with him.

"Better?" he breathed against her ear.

She nodded against his shoulder, aware that she was

stretching to accommodate him, twisting so that he could find his satisfaction—and she could find hers.

Her mouth, her cheek, her eyes, were in the hollow of his neck. She tasted and felt the perspiration of his efforts to bring her comfort. To claim her. To love her.

She sensed his tremorous need as his muscles tensed and love sounds ripped from between his clenched teeth. With her hips pinioned beneath him, he settled deep between her legs and spilled himself inside her.

He shuddered, his flesh going rock hard, then flaccid with relief.

"Oh, baby," he groaned, his weight coming down on her. A second slipped away. "I'm too heavy for you," he said, levering himself up from her chest, her belly.

"No. It's okay." She held him, trying to bring him closer.

"A minute. A minute more," he compromised, though the statement seemed more for his benefit than hers.

They lay joined, twined together.

Cupid looked over his shoulder, up at the ceiling, and smiled, imagining the pleasures to be hers for an eternity—or, as the justice of the peace had recited, for as long as they lived.

She sighed.

"Yes?"

"I'm okay."

He chuckled. "You keep saying that, but you're more than okay."

Her smile widened.

"You've got the nicest…" He didn't say the word aloud, but he lifted from her and his fingertip trailed over the curve of her breast.

Cupid ducked her head, so he wouldn't recognize her pleasure—or her embarrassment.

"Ah, yes. We may get to know every inch of this heart-shaped bed before this honeymoon is over," he warned.

She smiled at the ceiling, and thanked her lucky stars for finding him.

"Hold on," he instructed, lifting from her completely and rolling to her side.

Cupid murmured, reluctant to let him go. They lay face-to-face, both on their sides, stark naked. He traced the outline of her torso, the dip of her waist, the flare of her hip. Finally, he snagged a corner of the sheet and drew it over her protectively. "You are an incredibly beautiful woman," he admitted. "And I'm an incredibly lucky man."

She nuzzled the top of her head beneath his chin. "I find you incredibly beautiful, too, in different ways."

"But you've no one to compare me with."

"Isn't that the way it's supposed to be?"

He didn't answer, his lengthy silence sending a ripple of foreboding through her. "Maybe. But I wish you had told me," he said finally. "If I'd known you had never been with a man before, that you were a virgin, I would have done things differently. Maybe even this marriage thing would have been handled differently."

"How?" she asked. "How can you make perfect any better?"

"Cupid—don't." She stilled. "You should have told me. I figured you knew what you were getting into with me. That you had had other boyfriends, that you knew there was a compatible side, an everyday side, an intimate side."

"Having other boyfriends doesn't mean I'd be intimate with them."

"Look. This was a surprise I wasn't expecting, that's all."

"I can't believe this. You sound disappointed."

"No. No, never that. I'm just...being cautious, pragmatic."

"Why?"

He shrugged. "It stirs up deeper feelings, that's all."

Cupid gently rested the palm of her hand on his chest, as near as she possibly could to his heart. "It never occurred to me that you'd consider this a surprise, Burke," she said softly. "I've always done what I thought was right. I believed marrying you was right, and giving myself to you was right. I saved that part of me to give to the right man," she emphasized. Beneath her hand, she felt him wince. "Because I wanted a forever marriage, with that right and perfect man."

"Then you got the wrong guy," he muttered. "He isn't me...because I've never been the right and perfect man. I'm a hard man, one who didn't get his share of feelings. And I'm certainly not perfect. You're inclined to think that, because that's the way you want it to be."

Cupid went cold. She struggled to get air into her lungs. "You're saying I made the wrong choice?" she said finally, a catch in her voice.

Burke hesitated, and then his words came out in an earnest rush of brutal honesty. "I don't want to hurt you, Cupid. Honest to God, I don't." He swept her into his arms and held her. "But don't make me say things I can't. Don't make me feel things that aren't there. I've told you the truth, right from the beginning. And I don't expect it to change—not now and not in the future. I'll go only so far in this relationship, as far as I'm able. Only that far, and no further."

# *Chapter Thirteen*

They made love again the next morning, and Cupid's passion astonished Burke. It was so good.

Damn good, damn satisfying. She was uninhibited and sexy. And sweet, through and through. A romp under the sheets with her was like one mad, delirious discovery, one sizzling sensation after another.

If he'd been a smoking man, he'd have lit up afterward.

So they'd made love and—damn, he hated using that phrase, "making love," but what else was there? "Having sex" with Cupid just didn't seem right. None of the crude and lewd terms seemed to fit, not where she was concerned.

So they'd been "together" and they were going out for breakfast, to spend their first full day as man and wife. While she got ready, he thumbed through a magazine, not really seeing any of the pages, but thinking instead of how she looked, and felt, and tasted.

Cupid stepped out of the dressing room, self-consciously running her palms over her pant legs. "I suppose you're starved," she said.

"You're not?" *After that workout?* he silently, incredulously, asked himself. He tossed the magazine aside and met her in the middle of the room.

She lifted both shoulders, a little helplessly. "I...feel a little different. The thought of leaving this room, after everything we shared last night and this morning—" She broke off, gazing up at him with hopeful eyes. Suddenly, without invitation, she slid under his arm and looped her arms around his middle. "I want to be a good wife to you, Burke. I want you to know that."

He felt a lump form in the back of his throat, and tried to swallow over it. "We'll be good for each other," he managed to reply. "It'll work out."

"I really do want to make you happy," she repeated.

"You have. Hey," he joked feebly, "you found me a bride, didn't you? Even if you had to marry me yourself."

"I never really knew I could feel this close to another human being."

"We," he whispered, tipping his chin against her temple, "were about as close as you can get."

"Burke, I mean here—" she patted his chest "—where you care about people."

He didn't want to go there. He didn't want to talk about hearts and feelings and love. Yet it plagued him no end, thinking how she had brought her chaste, genuine feelings to the marriage bed and laid them before him. He might never be able to return her affection, her honesty. "Cupid," he reminded her, gently, "we're going to miss the breakfast buffet."

"Oh." Cupid feigned mild disappointment. "Silly

me. I should have known that the way to a man's heart is through his stomach.''

"What's that supposed to mean?"

"I only wanted to talk, and tell you how I felt. About last night. And you.''

"But I'm not good at uttering all these little sweet nothings—and you're making me feel guilty that I can't. We're married, we're going to be a family. We respect each other, we'll do the best by each other. It will be enough, Cupid. I promise.''

Cupid's feelings went from confusion to slow simmer. What about all the things he'd said last night, about her being incredibly beautiful, about not wanting to hurt her? Didn't any of that count? "Last night, you made me think you cared.''

"For God's sake, I do. But you knew this. You knew it before you ever said 'I do.' I told you what I wanted and what I was willing to give. I can give you a life, and children. Everything else is up for grabs.''

He was right, of course. About everything. Cupid had gone into this with her eyes wide open. She'd taken her chances. She'd thought she could lead him down the garden path and straight into paradise—yes, well, they'd been to paradise and back, and apparently it hadn't done any good.

She'd reasoned that when he was with her physically, that would put him in touch with his emotional side. She'd fantasized that he would actually come out and declare his love for her, when they were alone, together, in the heart-shaped bed.

"You're being honest, Burke,'' she said finally. "I can't fault you for that.'' Yet something in her heart ached, as if it were about to break. She'd thought, truly thought, that she could win him over.

She had imagined that her passion would be enough for the two of them.

Instead, he only became more adamant. His refusal to accept her love or return it would ultimately bring about her own destruction. She'd lose her powers, her gifts. It would only be a matter of time.

Burke Riley, Cupid realized, was a miscalculation of the highest degree.

Cupid loathed waiting at airports. She typically broke the tedious monotony by making matches. Today, however, she had some trepidation about exercising her powers.

Burke paused at the deli counter to get them sandwiches, and Cupid spotted an attractive woman, one dressed in comfortable heels, with a practical all-weather coat at her side. One glance told Cupid the woman had little life outside of her job.

Pity.

She scanned the waiting room, zeroing in on another traveler across the aisle. Same approximate age, complementary smile lines.

Neither one of them was married or committed, she knew. Her radar seemed extraordinarily sharp this morning. Almost intense. Like a power surge.

Okay, so she'd experiment and see what happened.

Intentionally choosing a seat beside the woman, Cupid waited a full minute before engaging her in small talk, about the flight, her work.

"Yes, I love my business trips to Denver," the woman, Yvonne, admitted. "I'd move there in a minute, if the opportunity ever came up."

To Cupid's delight, the male target across the aisle

chimed in. "My co-workers are willing to bite the bullet and take a pay cut, for a move to Denver," he said.

Cupid, on a roll, got the man's name in a record seventeen seconds. She pumped herself up, prepared to execute the introduction and make another match. "Jim, this is Yvonne Wright." Her voice went thick, honeyed. "Yvonne, meet Jim Martin."

Cupid smiled smugly, expecting another grand finale.

Instead, Yvonne peered at her strangely, as if to say, "What on earth are you introducing me to him for?"

Jim fiddled with his laptop and muttered, "Yeah, um, nice to meet'cha."

Nothing. Absolutely, positively nothing.

Sparks died. Electricity failed. The introduction was a total shutdown, a power failure of the greatest magnitude.

Cupid blinked and beat back a panic attack. "Do you, er, know each other?" she ventured. The fine hairs on her arms were starting to rise.

"No."

Yvonne looked at her suspiciously. "Should we?"

"I thought that, with you taking the same plane—"

"Hope you like turkey," Burke interrupted, coming up to hand Cupid a wax-paper-wrapped sandwich.

"Yes. Fine." She accepted the sandwich and figured it really didn't matter—the only thing she was eating was crow. Her targets—Jim and Yvonne—dived back into their work, avoiding her. Yvonne scribbled in a notebook, Jim turned on his laptop.

Cupid had never before failed at making a match. Never. Even in the academy she had impressed her professors and amazed her fellow St. Valentine students. She gaped at the couple as horror burrowed in, making her quake with fear over the loss of her powers.

Theoretically, there were only a few reasons for a match not to gel: a failure of the electrostatically lobo-charged hydrosphere, an articulation and speech patterns failure, or a personal relationship failure.

The conditions had been right; her delivery had been exact. That left only one explanation: she had been deemed unworthy of her station and stripped of all powers and entitlements.

By marrying Burke, she had entered into and accepted a loveless relationship. By compromising her gift, she would exist on a truly mortal level. She would know how the lovelorn pine and the lovesick languish, and on the most intimate of levels. It was her penance, for sacrificing all she had been given and all she had earned.

A sick feeling washed over her.

Cupid didn't believe this could happen. Not to her. She'd thought she could beat the system. She'd thought she could win over Burke, and have her life go on unscathed.

How wrong. How foolish. How absurd.

Burke, who had settled in beside her, offered her a paper napkin. "Aren't you hungry?" he asked, indicating her unopened sandwich.

Burke's features blurred. His deeply tanned coloring faded to chalk-white, while his eyes, arresting pinpoints of light, bored into her. His hair seemed to float like a dark cloud over his head.

She was having a phantasm. Cupid panicked. A phantasm occurred before the complete loss of powers.

Her world whirled and tilted. Reality as she knew it spun crazily out of control.

The message was clear. Burke would be the key to the rest of her committed life, to healing and unrest, to conflict and contentment. Even to restorative powers.

Her future was irrevocably tied to Burke. He was her destiny and she'd sacrificed all for him.

The realization was humbling. She had taken her gifts for granted. She had overestimated her powers. She had allowed her own selfish desires to rule her conscious thought.

She might never get any of her powers back. There was no way out.

"Cupid?" Burke prompted, concern etched in his brow. "What is it? You look like you've seen a ghost."

"A phantasm," she mumbled, shivering and growing intolerably cold. Her spine went stiff, started tingling, while an arctic blast seemed to sweep through her mind, whisking away all the warm, rosy-colored thoughts.

"What?"

Cupid jerkily ran a fingernail over a seam in the wrapped sandwich. She was trembling so bad her hands shook. "Finally," she revised, forcing the tremors to still. "Finally, it hit me—that I'm married. To you."

Burke's features came back into focus, sharply, enough for her to recognize the hurt in his dark, brooding eyes. "And you're wondering what you've just done?" he asked.

She took a deep, cleansing breath and mustered her strength. The physical response had begun to ebb. The cold had faded to a dull chill; sensation was beginning to return to her limbs, her fingers. "No," she answered bravely. "No, I'm thinking of all the things I want to do, need to do, to start our life together."

There was no other alternative, Cupid realized. All of her time, all of her energies had to be invested in Burke. The direction of her life had changed, and now Burke was the biggest part of it.

He might not love her now, but she would chisel away

at him, and they would forge a life together. "I'm afraid you're going to have to put up with me," she warned. "I can't cook, I can't sew and I don't know much about ranching. But I do know the difference between first class and special delivery. If that helps."

The corner of his mouth lifted sardonically, and for that Cupid was grateful. "I guess we have a lot to learn about each other, don't we?"

"More than you realize," she warned softly.


No one—not Cupid's parents, or her sister, Lysandra—was surprised Cupid had run off and gotten married. She was always impulsive, they said to friends and family—and always right.

They welcomed Burke with open arms, which, Cupid noted, discomfited him.

They did insist on a reception, however, at the VFW hall, and Cupid wore her wedding dress, and Burke stuck a carnation in the lapel of his western-cut suit jacket. Venus said a chicken and mashed potatoes buffet was only appropriate, after all the weddings they'd been invited to. Her father hired Earl Munley's five-piece band and they all danced till two in the morning.

It was an event that bound them in the eyes of the community. No one thought anything about it when Cupid quit her job and put her house on the market. Of course, there were a few lame jokes that the Valentine post office would never be as sweet, nor as romantic, without Cupid in it.

They settled into a comfortable life, Burke and Cupid. She admired his sprawling ranch house, and marveled at the big, spacious rooms. There were four oversize bedrooms, and cavernous connecting hallways. It was a man's house, to be sure—right down to the threadbare carpets and the worn furniture—but she put her own distinctive touches to it, then added some of her own things to the mix.

The most remarkable thing, Burke admitted one night, were the stars Cupid put on the ceiling in the master bedroom. She reminded him how he'd mentioned missing the stars in Las Vegas, and he'd looked at her, visibly affected, then brushed it off, saying he was surprised she'd remembered.

"I remember everything you say, Burke," she said. They were getting ready for bed, and his hand stopped working the snaps on his shirt. "Does that surprise you?"

"Kind of, yes."

Cupid moved across the room to him and looped her arms about his middle. "You like it, don't you?"

"Yeah." He glanced up at all the little fluorescent sticky stars scattered across his ceiling. His old man would have poked fun at this silliness, for sure. Cupid had even duplicated some of the constellations—the Big Dipper, the Milky Way. "I'm even getting used to the hearts in the kitchen," he allowed. "'Course, the hands don't know where to wash up anymore, worried they'll get your pink towels dirty."

She laughed. "Are you saying I'm making a mess of your life?"

He gazed down at her thoughtfully. "I'm saying this ranch has never seen so many hearts and flowers. Sometimes I look around and figure I fell into someone else's life."

Cupid tipped her head in mock horror. "What? Are you saying you don't like it?"

"Nope. Just getting used to the softness, is all."

It was all he'd had to say to convince Cupid that she

was making progress. She merely had to acclimate the man, tenderize his heart, his thoughts, his soul. Cupid threw herself into making the house a warm, welcoming place. She made best friends with Burke's dog, Laddie, then made noises about getting a kitten.

Burke frowned. "Warm-blooded creatures of the feline variety usually don't stick around here," he said. At Cupid's disappointed look, he added, "Besides, I'm allergic." Yet within the week, he'd brought home a basketful of kittens, and taken Cupid out to the barn to see them. "Barn cats," he said, dismissing the gesture. "Good mousers."

The gardens had gone untended for decades, yet Cupid saw possibilities and planned a strategy to put things in order again. She attacked with a vengeance.

"What's this?" she asked Burke's grizzly old ranch hand one balmy morning as she pulled a profusion of weeds from the side gardens.

"Bleeding heart," he answered. "The missus put it in years ago, when she and Burke's daddy were still on speaking terms. The stuff just went wild after she left."

*Bleeding heart?* Cupid shuddered and stared at the dried leaves in her hand. A bad sign. Her mother refused to plant bleeding heart in her garden, and claimed it was like asking for trouble. "And yet it still grows, after all these years?" Cupid mused.

He lifted a shoulder. "I recollect how the old man threw a little fertilizer on it there for a spell. Kind of like the last thing he had to remind him of the missus. Said these gardens were nothing but a nuisance, but he never said to spade 'em under, either. Kind of liked to grouse about 'em, as I recall." He paused. "You want, I can spade it under for you."

Cupid debated, then shook her head. "No. Not yet."

As he ambled away, Cupid pensively crumbled the leaves between her fingers, and automatically repeated her mantra. The bits tumbled away on the gusting March wind.

She'd leave the plant in, she decided impulsively. It was a link to Burke's troubled past, and there was a reason for it. Perhaps love had lived here once. Perhaps it had never been nurtured, not enough to truly thrive...only enough to survive.

Cupid worked on the gardens every chance she got, and in between she worked on other mundane things.

She cleaned out Burke's freezer and found a place for the top layer of their wedding cake. Cupid had always drawn a clear line between superstitions, old wives' tales and tradition. While she didn't believe in the former, she did put some stock in the latter. Eating the cake, she figured, was a tradition they should enjoy on their first anniversary.

She hung curtains, embellished with roses, in the guest bedroom. She dragged Burke's overstuffed leather chair, and his collection of coffee-table books depicting the American West, from the far corner of their bedroom to near the window. Two weeks later, she invested in a down comforter, pillow shams, a fleece throw and Egyptian cotton sheets that were as soft and comforting as sweet butter.

"What have you done?" he asked, as he slid, bare-butt naked, between the sheets.

"I learned how to dress a bed," Cupid announced proudly. "Do you know there's a formula for it at the store?"

He chuckled and unfolded his arm, so she could curl up next to him and put her head on his shoulder. "Funny, I always figured you undressed for bed."

It was true. Cupid rarely spent time in her nightgown in Burke's bedroom. It was the best time of day. The togetherness, the pillow talk, the staring up at stars on the inky, blue-black ceiling. The other intimate, passionate things they shared at night.

Yet even with the magic of their nights, during the day Cupid witnessed Burke's distancing. She saw the little ways he protected his heart, how he pushed himself around the ranch, how he gave himself over to the tough rancher image. Often his words were clipped, his demeanor abrupt.

It was as if there were two halves of him, the one she discovered at night and the one she lived with during the day.

Yet she frequently caught him watching her, as if smitten with the strangest fascination. He anticipated her needs, making sure the gas tank on her car was filled, or opening the pickle jar before she could struggle with it.

It was midnight on a Friday when he chuckled and pensively stroked a pensive path down her arm with the pad of his thumb. "You ate the last pickle in the jar again."

"I know."

Cupid relished the sensations his fingertips made on her bare arm. This was the prelude, she thought dizzily, before he started kissing her.

Her breasts, though sore and tender, craved his attention.

Cupid went taut, her breasts burgeoned and strained beneath her thin gown, and need spiraled right down through her middle, igniting a quick fire at the juncture of her legs.

This was the way it started, with small talk and caresses, before they coupled…and loved.

"I need to get groceries tomorrow," she said, stretching catlike against his body. "Pickles, ice cream…that sort of thing. Want to come along?"

"Got to get that filly over to Mierson's tomorrow," he said. "Can't."

She went on without skipping a beat. "Oh. Too bad. I wanted to get another home pregnancy kit, just to make sure. Before going to the doctor."

He stilled. "What?"

She rolled on her side, purposely letting her belly rub against him. "It would seem, Mr. Riley, that we're having a baby."

"You're pregnant?"

"That surprises you? After all the time we've spent trying to?" Cupid smiled in the dark and swiped the tip of her tongue against his shoulder, remembering nights filled with earnest, passionate thrusts, every one designed to put him closer to her heart. She had brought him into herself, welcoming him, and found sheer joy doing so.

"I—I didn't think it would happen this quickly."

"It probably happened on our wedding night," she confided, burrowing the top of her head against his flesh, "or right after."

Instead of stroking her arm, his hand tightened around her biceps, and his muscles tensed. "We're plunging into this family thing right away then."

"It would seem so. I'll get a date from the doctor…but I think by Thanksgiving you'll be a daddy."

He snorted. "Huh."

She put her palm on his breastbone and ran her fingertips through the curling hair on his chest. "It's a rea-

son to celebrate, Burke,'' she said, imagining he'd sweep
her into his arms, and they'd experience one more heady
night of lovemaking.

He nodded. ''We'll do dinner, tomorrow night.'' His
arm tightened, securing her in an embrace.

Cupid's breasts were full and tight against his side.
''Mmm, yes,'' she agreed, repositioning herself at a
more comfortable angle.

He released her slightly. ''Are you sore?'' he asked,
sliding a hand down the curve of her breast and over her
middle.

''A little.''

''I don't want to hurt you.''

''You won't.''

Burke didn't say anything, not for a moment. Then he
mused, ''Life's funny, isn't it? You get what you wish
for, then you don't quite know what to do with it, do
you?''

Cupid guessed at the significance of his words. Cowboy colloquialisms, she called them. Accompanied with
actions louder than words. Burke struggled to express
his happiness, to tell her how much this event, the birth
of their baby, would mean to him. She'd promised herself to give him all the time he needed, to learn how to
express the emotions that bound a man and a woman, to
feel confident in the trust they shared.

Cupid considered how her life had changed. She had
a husband now, and soon a baby. Her old life was over,
her powers long absent. ''We have a lot to look forward
to,'' she said, refusing to regret any of her choices.

Burke didn't reply, but he held her for a long time in
silence, and that night, for the first time since their wedding night, they didn't make love.

# *Chapter Fourteen*

Even as she grew bigger, and rounder every day, and more enamored of her pregnancy, a part of Cupid began to erode. Burke was changing, and she didn't know how to stop it from happening.

Her family was thrilled that they'd have another baby in the family, but Burke grew grim, as if the responsibilities of a wife and a family were wearing him down. Cupid didn't understand it. Not at all. It was what he wanted.

On occasion, he did talk about the baby, convinced they were having a boy.

Yet as the days grew longer, he worked longer hours away from the house. Some days she rarely saw him, and he'd drop into bed beside her hours after she'd fallen asleep.

Cupid was perplexed, disappointed. True, it was the busiest time of year for a rancher, but this was not the marriage she'd envisioned. It was as if he purposely found reasons to be away from her. On her worst days she wondered if he was repulsed by her widening girth.

"We have an invitation from my folks for a Fourth of July picnic," she said one evening, as she put Burke's favorite meal, a roast with all the trimmings, on the table.

"Can't. Got to get that hay in. You go ahead if you want."

"Burke? Surely you can take one day off. The weather's been nothing but perfect, and the forecast for the next week is—"

"I just cut another eighty acres. Can't let it lie in the field, in case we get rain."

"It's a holiday!"

"So?"

"So you haven't wanted to do anything for the last two months. Not with me. Not with my family. Not with anyone."

He tossed his napkin beside his plate. "You tryin' to pick a fight?"

"I'm trying to figure out what's going on!"

"Nothing's going on. I've got hay to bring in, that's what!" he shouted.

Tears pricked Cupid's eyes, but she wouldn't give in to them. She wouldn't! She was emotional because of the pregnancy, that was all. "Yes. And ever since I've said we're having a baby you've been busy!" she exclaimed.

"This is a ranch. A *working* ranch," he retorted. "I don't put things on hold because a holiday rolls around. Or because my wife's having a baby."

"Gee," she said sarcastically, "do you think you'll have to time to show up when your wife's having that baby?" A muscle in his jaw thumped wickedly, and his gray gaze glittered. "Or should I schedule a time when you aren't hauling feed, or taking stock to market, or cleaning out the barns?"

"Maybe I made a mistake," he said, through clenched teeth. "Maybe I should have introduced you to my life, so you knew what a rancher does."

"A rancher," Cupid said, without thinking, "may work long hours during the day, but at night he makes love to his wife." Cupid, horrified, slapped her hand over her mouth, wondering where that had come from.

Still, it was true. He hadn't made love to her for a month.

He stared at her. "Is that what this is about?"

"I..." she didn't want to back down. "I don't know. Partly. It's about everything, I guess. I..." She trailed off, afraid to be honest, but knowing she had no other choice. "I miss you. I married you because I wanted to be with you."

He grimaced, his eyelids going half-mast. "I want you in my bed," he said, his voice gravelly, "but...I don't want anything to happen to the baby...or you...."

"You're worried something will happen to the baby?" Her hand involuntarily reached out to pluck at his sleeve. "Our life in the bedroom can go on as it did before. The doctor said so." Burke didn't reply, going tight-lipped, grim. "You don't believe me?"

He shrugged. "It's only a little while till the baby's born, and after that—"

It dawned on her then. His feelings, his emotions were tied to the baby. Not to her. He had meant what he said—that he'd never really love her. He'd wanted her to have his children, wanted to use her like the studs used the mares on a working ranch. The thought made her physically sick.

She rose to leave the table, but Burke's hand circled her wrist like a band of iron. "I want you in my bed," he repeated. "What's it going to take to convince you?"

She gazed at him, experiencing a crazy mixture of shock and weariness and confusion all rolled into one. Tears pricked the corners of her eyes, and she bit her lower lip so hard a tiny drop of blood glistened.

He swore, and she jerked back.

"I don't want to hurt you, Cupid," he said hoarsely. "I never have." He released her wrist and stood, towering over her, looking down at her with the most indecisive expression on his face. He whisked his thumb over her lower lip. "You bit yourself so hard, you drew blood," he muttered.

"Redheads," she choked out. "We have thin skin."

His laugh was harsh, but empathetic. "You're unhappy." It was a statement, not a question.

She shook her head. "I just want my husband back."

Pain rolled through his flinty eyes. "I don't know if you can ever really have him," he said. "I don't."

He kissed her then, long and hard, before he swept her up in his arms and carried her into the bedroom. He placed her on the bed as if she was fragile, and trailed a hand over her rounding tummy. He eased her clothes off, but recklessly tore at his, kicking them aside before he joined her on the soft down comforter.

Their lovemaking was passionate, intense. Afterward, Cupid lay entwined in his arms.

"Does this mean you're coming to the Fourth of July picnic?" she said.

"Of course," he said simply, reaching to protectively draw a sheet over her cooling, perspiration-damp body.

Cupid let her eyes drift closed, reveling in his ministrations. Maybe she had misunderstood. Perhaps his responsibilities with the ranch were truly more than she had imagined. No one this tender, this considerate, could be intentionally cruel.

"I don't ever want to fight with you, Cupid," he said softly. "Not like what happened tonight."

"I know. Me neither."

"If it comes to that, and you think it isn't going to work out," he said, "I want you to know you're free to leave." Cupid froze. "But the baby stays here," Burke added. "He's my son and he belongs here, with me, on this ranch. You'll promise me that?"

Cupid, stunned by his proclamation, nodded dumbly. It was a silly promise, she reasoned later, during the sleepless hours of the night, because she had no intention of leaving Burke. She had every intention of taming him.

Burke felt like a heel. He'd been irascible and he knew it. He did cut his hours back and he spent more time with Cupid, but he couldn't beat back the fear. That she'd leave him. That she'd grow restless of the monotony of their life on the ranch. That she'd move on to greener pastures.

He wasn't a lovable man, and he knew it.

His mother had had little time for him, and had left without much of a backward glance. Even now she was busy with her own life, and had barely recognized his marriage. She'd sent a card, with a check.

His father had routinely dispensed harsh punishment, but few kind words. Burke's childhood had been a pull-yourself-up-by-your-bootstraps existence. It had made him strong and self-reliant, and it had served him well, teaching him survival.

Now things were different. Now Burke was having all these second thoughts, and regrets, and what-might-have-been moments. There were days he knew he hadn't been prepared for the softer, gentler side of life.

He had other days when he feared he was truly his father's son and drifting in the direction genetics had shaped for him: as a cantankerous old cuss who was scared as hell his wife would run off with someone better, younger, smarter, to someplace nicer, warmer, more hospitable.

Burke had fought being like his old man all his life, and he'd thought he'd won—until Cupid came along. He wanted to keep her with him so badly that the pent-up fears multiplied. With her, he knew everything he had to lose.

It wasn't just the baby. It was *her*. God, he didn't know what he'd do if he ever lost her. He couldn't say he loved her. Hell, he hadn't been brought up to know what love even was. He'd never really experienced it himself. Half the time he figured he wasn't capable of loving anybody or anything, as if that part of him had been sliced right out, at the most vulnerable time of his childhood. But he cared for Cupid, and he couldn't imagine a life without her.

He guessed that was why he was holding his unborn baby hostage, and why he'd said what he had. He knew that Cupid would never leave him, not if it meant leaving her baby behind. He had witnessed it himself, all those maternal instincts in her as she hovered on the wings of motherhood.

He would watch her pat her rounding stomach, and he'd go weak and warm on the inside. He would catch her talking to the baby, and he'd do all he could to go unnoticed, so he could hear her croon and carry on with their son.

The colors she chose for the nursery, teal blues and

pale pinks, crimped a bit of the indifference in his surly heart. The books she chose for the shelves, illustrated copies of nursery rhymes, made him ignore the *Quarter Horse Journal* and the stock market report. Instead he'd flip the pages of *Mother Goose* as if he were placating Cupid, when in fact he was satiating his own curiosity. The tiny clothes she arranged in the dresser—itty-bitty pajama sleepers not much bigger than the palm of his hand, booties as big as his thumb, blankets as soft as lamb's wool—fascinated him. Combined, they all put a crease in his attitude.

Like maybe there was something bigger than what he'd first believed about this marriage and family thing. That it was all-encompassing, and too big and unwieldy for him to control.

His home wasn't his own anymore. It was filled with pink hearts and red roses, and the scent of baking sugar cookies. He had this redheaded little vixen in his bed who had started wearing a black silk pajama top, with Hers embroidered on the pocket, because it was the only thing that fit.

He liked it. All of it. But he didn't know how to just come out and say it.

He didn't know when he started feeling guilty. He just knew he did.

He'd been honest with Cupid about one thing, and he'd meant it: he never wanted to hurt her. But he had. With making her promise about the baby. By pushing her away because the words stuck in his throat. By acting like he didn't care about all her efforts to keep the house, earn the respect of his ranch hands, make herself visible every day on the ranch.

Cupid was the kindest, gentlest woman he had ever known. Yet she was changing, right before his eyes, and he didn't have any explanation for it. No explanation but himself and his behavior. It wasn't the pregnancy, he knew that.

She didn't seem to be herself anymore. It was if she were distracted. She no longer pressed him about love, or the importance of making commitments to others and to the world.

Hell, she didn't even talk about setting people up anymore. She used to say, 'Oh, they'd be a good match for each other. We should do something about that.'''

He remembered a time when she'd wanted to make people happy, as if it was her nature or something. Now he wasn't even so sure about that. He wasn't disappointed by it. He didn't feel as if she was letting him down or anything. No. It was more like he was letting her down. As if he'd somehow clipped her wings. As if he had somehow smothered the life out of her.

The fire in her eyes was gone. The glow was absent.

It worried him.

Hell's bells, expectant mothers were supposed to glow, weren't they?

It was peculiar, this living together, being man and wife. The more he worried about her, the more he couldn't talk to her. He was afraid he'd make things worse, afraid he'd drive her away.

He'd even started stopping in at the tavern on the way out of Thurlby, just to avoid going home to her—to the place he most wanted to be. It made no sense, none of it. He felt like his old man all over again. He'd shoot a game of pool and have a couple of beers, and he'd look deep into the glass and imagine accusation on Cupid's features.

He just couldn't give her what she wanted, dammit! She wanted him to love her—and that was never ever part of the bargain.

Things had been rough, and Cupid was discouraged. She tried not to show it, but sometimes Burke's silence was too much to bear. She could almost feel him pussy-footing around her, as if he wanted to avoid her. Either that, or worse, making her feel like she was a broodmare under observation.

Passion, she observed wryly, had been so fleeting.

Love, it appeared, was elusive.

At least on his side.

He was such a good, good man. But it nagged at Cupid that he could not accept that goodness in himself. There were moments when she felt as if she were nurturing him, as well as their unborn baby. It was not the way she wanted her marriage to be.

She wanted to meet him on equal ground, to be a helpmate during the day and a lover at night. Instead, he didn't appear to need her help, not for anything. He admonished her about working too hard in the gardens, and he reluctantly praised all she'd accomplished with the house.

She didn't need the praise. It wasn't that. It was the sharing she missed—and she didn't know how to get it back.

Her mother had suspected something was amiss, and had carefully broached the subject with her. Not to worry, Venus said, men sometimes felt displaced by their firstborn, as if they were losing their wife to motherhood.

Cupid smiled bravely through the advice, vaguely wondering if her mother knew, too, that she'd lost her powers.

"You haven't made a match lately, have you?" Venus inquired unexpectedly one afternoon.

Cupid blanched. She couldn't tell her mother that she had knowingly married a man who didn't love her. She couldn't. It was out of the realm of possibility. Her mother would never recover from such a blunder. Venus was stoic and resilient, but she drew the line at jeopardizing her powers. She'd never be able to fathom how Cupid, her own daughter, had done so. Venus and her father were hopelessly in love. "Oh, I—I've been considering doing more calculated matches. Like Lysandra. It makes more sense. Out here."

Her mother nodded. "What's Burke think about that?"

"Well…" Cupid hedged, her voice rising. "I haven't told him. Not exactly. I've sort of alluded to the fact that—"

"Cupid."

"Mom, everything's happened so fast. Give the guy a break."

"Cupid, darling. If he loves you, he's certainly going to understand." *If he loves you.* That was the catch. Those were the key words. "Your daddy," Venus confided, "thought he'd stumbled onto something pretty darn special when he found out what my side of the family brought to the marriage." She patted Cupid's hand. "Now don't worry so. Burke just has the new-daddy jitters. He doesn't want to share you, that's all. I'm the one to worry, seeing these circles under your eyes."

Cupid smiled bravely and discounted the suggestion that Burke was jealous of the baby. It wasn't that. Not at all. It was something deeper, more profound.

The rift between them grew wider. The days slipped away, and they moved closer to her due date.

Cupid sought resolution before she gave birth to their child. One more little person, with his own set of demands, would change the dynamics of their relationship all over again. She couldn't bear thinking about it. She could hardly bear anything these days.

She wondered idly if this was what it was to be lovesick, this mooning around, this unsettled, unfulfilled sensation that crept into her being.

She wanted no more complications, no more distress. She only wanted Burke. If she wanted him, truly, she needed to do something, she decided resolutely one afternoon. To earn his love, and security for her baby—and to get her powers back—she had to take action.

Cupid put her plan in motion at 5:00 a.m. on a Tuesday morning, before Burke had time to slip away to the barns.

In his stocking feet, he stopped dead in his tracks in the middle of the kitchen floor. "You're up?"

It wasn't even light outside yet. "You came in late last night and I wanted to catch you before you went out this morning." A guilty look crossed his face. She knew why, and she guessed where he'd been. The tavern outside of Thurlby. He'd crawled into bed at midnight, smelling of beer and stale cigarette smoke. She lifted the skillet. "Eggs?"

"Um, yeah. That'd be fine. If it's no trouble."

"No trouble." She worked silently while he sat down and slipped into his boots.

"I, um, ran into an old friend from Thurlby last night and he wanted to catch up a little," he said, as a matter of explanation.

"Oh." She kept her back to him, poking at the eggs with the turner.

Burke heaved a sigh, then rose from the chair and crossed the kitchen, looping both arms around her widening middle. "I suppose I should have called," he half apologized. "I wanted to call, but I was worried I'd wake you. Figure you need your rest and all."

She gave the eggs a good poke. "It wouldn't have mattered, whether you called or not, because I wasn't able to sleep." She left the rest unsaid.

"You should be in bed now, instead of up doing this. I know you tire easily."

She flipped the eggs over. "I just can't get comfortable anymore." She shrugged. "Not sitting, not standing, not even lying down. But it won't be much longer."

His hands moved up her shoulders, giving her a light squeeze. "About last night?" he said hesitantly, "I'd rather have been here with you."

This was her opening, and Cupid pounced on it. She turned off the burner, slid the eggs onto the plate and put the turner aside. "You can make it up to me," she suggested, pivoting to face him.

"Okay. How?"

"The doctor wants to do an ultrasound this morning at ten. Come with me."

He pulled back as if he was trapped, and started backpedaling. "I—that's only—" he looked at the clock "—a few hours away."

"I mentioned it last week."

He drew a ragged breath. "Cupid. I wouldn't fit in, not sitting in a waiting room full of pregnant females. I'd just be in the way, and—"

"And you're making excuses."

A second slipped away. "Yeah. Because..."

"Burke, I need you there with me. I'm a little scared." *Lie.* She wasn't, not at all. But she'd resort to doing or saying anything to draw him into the web of love she intended to weave. "I know it sounds silly. But I look at you sometimes and see pure strength…" Now that part was true. If he could only temper that strength with love. "Knowing you were there, beside me, would make me stronger, too. Hey, we could slip you in the back door if it made you feel better."

He waffled.

"We made this baby together," she said softly, capturing his hand and placing it on her abdomen. "But you haven't even heard your baby's heartbeat yet." She paused, aware when the baby moved beneath his hand. "Punch Riley might not have been in the delivery room when his wife delivered his son. But you're not Punch Riley. You told me. You're doing things different this time around."

Burke swallowed, his jaw firming and his eyes squeezing closed. He gave in, asking only one question. "What time do we leave?"

# Chapter Fifteen

Burke heard the *whoosh-whoosh* of the baby's heart-beat, witnessed the blurry depiction of their baby on the ultrasound monitor. His heart leaped to his throat. His chest grew full and hard, yet he couldn't get any air in his lungs.

Flailing arms and legs. So tiny. So helpless.

Somewhere behind his Adam's apple, a knot grew. He tried to swallow and couldn't.

Cupid wriggled her hand into his palm, and he clasped it, holding on for dear life. My God. This was one little adventure they'd created together and would have to see through to completion. He was smitten, physically unable to drag his eyes away from the screen.

"Why, that's strange," the lab technician said, adjusting the screen and probing through the gel she'd smeared over Cupid's belly. Jelly belly, the tech had teased earlier. "I'm getting a pinkish cast."

Cupid's eyes flew open.

"I don't know," the tech commented, "must be the morning light."

Cupid lifted imperceptibly off the examining table, her head swiveling to the screen so she could see better.

"Is this your first ultrasound?"

"Yes," Cupid answered breathlessly. A new feeling of hope, of euphoria, blossomed inside her.

"This is really strange. Really. I haven't ever had anything like this before."

Burke frowned, then slanted a dubious look at Cupid.

"It's not the imaging," the tech added, "it's like it's the screen." She tapped the glass. "See? It's almost like—"

"Maybe it's a reflection," Cupid interrupted, "off my jacket."

They all glanced at Cupid's red fleece jacket, which hung on a hook next to the window.

Burke's gray gaze clouded thoughtfully.

The tech made a move to adjust the blinds, then stopped. "Aw, heck," she said, plopping back down on the stool, "maybe it's the equipment. It's probably on the fritz again."

The pink aura remained onscreen. Cupid shot a look in Burke's direction and recognized a hint of suspicion. "So, everything's fine otherwise?" she asked, trying to distract them both.

The tech smiled. "I'm not a doctor, but it looks to me like you're going to have a healthy baby. She's— whoops—" The tech bit off the sentence, probing Cupid's belly for a better view. "I'm sorry. Did you want to know what sex it is?" she asked cautiously.

"A girl," Burke said incredulously, dropping Cupid's hand. "It's a girl?"

"I'm sorry," the tech apologized to Cupid, "I didn't

mean to ruin the surprise for you or your husband. I could be wrong, though.''

"It's all right," Cupid assured her. "Don't worry about it.''

"No. Wait.'' Burke leaned over her belly to get a better look at the screen. "That can't be right. There's some mistake. We're having a boy.''

The tech laughed at his adamant pronouncement. "I'll admit that this prediction is by guess and by golly, Mr. Riley, but in this case, I really think—''

"No,'' he said decisively. "We're having a boy.''

"Burke.'' Cupid's hand fluttered to his chest, to remind him that they had no choice in the matter, to bring him back to reality.

It didn't do any good. His face fell, and he was obviously disappointed. "But what am I going to do with a girl?'' he asked, poleaxed.

They rode in silence for the first fifteen miles after they left the doctor's office. The next ten miles were crucial, Cupid realized, because they would give her just enough time to say what she needed to.

Burke was a captive audience, here in the car. He couldn't avoid her; he couldn't turn away. He had to listen.

"Well, Burke,'' she said, staring straight ahead through the windshield, "it looks like I've failed on all counts.''

"I don't know what you're talking about.''

"Yes, you do. Don't you even dare try to weasel out on me like that,'' she said. "I can make other people fall in love, but I can't make you love me. I can give you a daughter—this time around—but I can't give you a son.''

"It doesn't matter," he said brusquely, turning on the radio.

She waited until he pulled his hand away, then snapped it back off. "Oh, yes, it matters. It matters a lot to you. You'll never convince me otherwise. I saw your expression in there. You were disappointed. It was written all over you. And you made me feel like I'd failed. I'd failed you, failed this marriage—"

"Would you stop?" He clenched the steering wheel, his voice rising.

"What? I suppose you think this is another fight!"

"Well? Isn't it?"

"I don't know what it is anymore, Burke. The more I try to make you happy, the more I seem to fail." Defeat permeated every bone in her body, but she refused to give in to it.

"You haven't failed me," he muttered. "But I swear to God I don't know what's happened to you. You've changed. You want more from me than you did six months ago, or nine months ago, or—"

"*I've* changed?" She let the question hang midair. Then she patted her tummy. "You're right. On all counts."

His foot rode a little heavy on the accelerator.

"Slow down," she demanded.

He took a deep breath and eased the car back to the speed limit.

"Yes, I've changed," she said finally, her voice breaking. "You made me a woman, Burke. I waited a lifetime for you. I gave myself to you because I wanted to. I *chose* to. You gave me a child, one that I carry next to my heart, every minute of every day." His eyes fluttered closed. When he opened them they were glassy, hard. "But most of all, I gave you my love...and you have refused to accept it."

Burke winced visibly, but his eyes remained fastened on the narrow ribbon of asphalt stretching ahead of them. "You're getting yourself all upset," he said. "It's not good for you, or for the baby."

"I am not getting myself all upset," she spat back irrationally. "Everything around us is upset. Our marriage is upset."

"So it's not the sweet little lovebird marriage you envisioned. I told you from the beginning that there's a limit to my feelings. These proclamations of love and all that hooey, none of it means anything!"

"It doesn't?"

"People make false declarations all the time. Probably half the people sitting in that chapel waiting to get married last February 14 are already divorced by now, or in the process of it."

"You suppose?" Cupid replied wryly.

"Okay! So it wasn't the wedding you envisioned, either!"

She swiveled on the seat indignantly. "And I told you, Burke, it's none of that, but what we brought to the marriage. I wouldn't have married you if I didn't want to."

"And I wouldn't be here right now if I didn't want to be, either," he said just as quickly. "I might not make extravagant declarations, but I'm here, and I'll be here. For a long, long time to come. Maybe our marriage won't last forever. But I'll stick around for the baby. And I'd think you'd want to, too."

Cupid gnawed her lower lip and studied the gravel on the floor mats.

Seeing a chink in her composure, Burke pressed his

advantage. "C'mon. We're arguing over nothing. None of this means anything. We both want the same thing for our baby."

"It's more than the baby, Burke. What about us?"

"What about us?"

"It's our marriage. It's the foundation of our life together, and it's crumbling away under our feet."

The blood in his veins turned cold, desperate. "Okay, so maybe it won't last forever. But we should be able to make it last long enough to raise this baby together. Lots of people have an in-name-only marriage." Cupid's jaw slid off center. "Just like some people have a public and a private side. He goes his way, she goes hers."

Cupid stared at him in disbelief. All of the last year of poignant memories she'd collected dissolved, going *poof!* in her head.

He'd won.

He was stronger, more determined, more headstrong than she was. He refused to relinquish his heart, and no matter what she did, she couldn't win him over.

They were less than a mile from the ranch, and he purposely slowed the car.

"I don't think you understand something," she said, a catch in her voice and a sheen in her eyes. "I love you." Cupid slowly, carefully enunciated the last three words, enhancing them with the honeyed tone that once, so long ago, had worked on all of her matches. "And I love your baby, too. I love you both too much to do that to either of you."

He turned into the drive. She could hear his heart pounding at a maddening speed as he inched through the gate. "Cupid, we can work this out."

He pulled up by the front door, shielding the car from the barns, the bunkhouse. Cupid figured the last thing he wanted was to be interrupted by his ranch hands, not when he was in the middle of working things out with his wife.

She waited until he turned off the engine. "No, we can't," she said slowly. "We can't work this out. We let it go too far. I thought I could give you time, but it came at my expense." She shook her head. "I've lost so many things, Burke. You have no idea. I don't even know who I am anymore."

"Cupid—" He put a hand on her arm, but she shook it off and clambered out of the car.

Even with her ungainly gait, she walked up to the front door with dignity. He was on her heels and opened it for her, letting her precede him.

She stood in the middle of the cavernous living room and dropped her purse on the coffee table. She kicked off her shoes. "I'm tired, Burke. I'm tired of absolutely everything."

He grabbed a frilly, heart-shaped pillow and put it at the end of the couch. "Here. Lie down," he said solicitously. "You'll feel better."

In spite of the dire situation, in spite of her frustration, Cupid looked at the forlorn, thin little pillow he'd arranged, and laughed. Too little, too late.

Her mother claimed some men never got the message until you hit them over the head with it. Maybe Burke was one of those, and here all along Cupid had been thinking he was nothing but stubborn. No, he was just dense. Too dense to realize how much she loved him, too dense to realize what he was going to lose.

"No, Burke, thank you, I'm not that kind of tired." She shook her head and started for the hallway leading to the bedrooms. "I need some time away. To think about what I want. Out of this life, out of the marriage."

She turned back, offering him a shaky smile as she lifted a shoulder. "Who knows? Maybe to find some of the things I've lost. Maybe I'll rediscover them. Maybe I'll find a way to live with you—and if I can't, I'll find a way to live without you."

# Chapter Sixteen

A new conviction rose in Cupid. She'd laid her love before him. She'd told him clearly, in no uncertain terms, that she loved him. What more was there for her to do?

She'd given him the opportunity and he couldn't bring himself to respond to her.

The one thing about leaving, she thought dismally, was that her bag was already half-packed. She pulled it out of the closet and tossed it on the bed, unzipping it.

There were all the special things she'd purchased for her hospital stay. The new pink gown, the slippers. She pushed everything aside and pulled clothes from their hangers, letting the hangers bang against the wall and create an awful, hollow noise.

Cupid stared at the vacancy she'd created. It had always bothered her how empty closets looked when they were cleaned out. It bothered her more now. The hanger marks on the walls seemed to jeer at her, pointing out her failures, her inadequacies. A big hollow space, where her clothes had hung next to his.

Nothing but a big hollow space.

Just like her heart.

The thought went rolling through her head just as a clutching pain gripped her middle.

Cupid drew a ragged breath and sat back on the edge of the bed. Her shoulders hunched and she grabbed her rounded belly. The pain was gone as quickly as it came.

"Whoa," she said with a shudder. Maybe Burke was right, she admitted. Maybe she shouldn't go getting herself all upset. She had a few weeks to go.

She stood, but suddenly felt shaky, as if her legs wouldn't support her.

It was the feverish pitch of emotions, the upheaval, the whacky hormones of pregnancy, she told herself. So she paced herself, putting a lid on her frenetic activity and folding her clothes methodically, cramming the suitcase as full as she possibly could.

Cupid slammed the suitcase closed as another pain crunched up through her middle, squeezing the breath out of her. Shutting her eyes, she bent double.

Counting to ten, and waiting until the pain subsided, she straightened again, then fumbled with the zipper on the suitcase, vaguely wondering if this was such a good idea.

She wavered. Maybe she should think this over. Maybe she shouldn't walk out on Burke now. Especially not when she felt so vulnerable.

Besides, if she made such a monumental decision, there might be no going back. He was a hard man, not given to concessions.

She didn't want to lose him, not over one hasty moment, or one irrational act.

From her subconscious another thought rose up, offering the single argument that would incite her to walk out the door. *He didn't love her; he'd never love her.*

Cupid yanked the suitcase off the bed and headed for the car.

With his back to her, Burke stared out the front picture window. His boots were planted in the plush carpet, his hands behind his back, his shoulders rigid. She walked around him and out onto the front porch. Instead of lumbering down the steps, she took them nimbly, angrily. Jerking open the car door, she flung her suitcase in the back seat.

Behind her, she heard Burke's boots chewing up the gravel. He was hell-bent for leather and right on her tail.

"And where is it you think you're going?" he demanded.

Cupid whirled, ready to let him have a very big piece of her mind—but life interfered. A new life. It was very determined, and not to be ignored.

The baby did a somersault—a loop-the-loop—and a tiny spurt of warm liquid soaked the inside seams of Cupid's slacks. It trickled down her leg. The subsequent rhythmic release of water made her hesitate.

She shifted uncertainly, then looked down at her feet. Dark stains soaked her socks, her shoes.

*Her water had broken.*

"Well?" he prompted.

Cupid looked over the trunk of the car at him, dazed. This was the father of her child. This was the man who said he'd pulled dozens of calves at birth, but privately admitted that he was a little bit skittish about being in a delivery room at the hospital. He figured he'd be in the way. He didn't see how he could be of any help.

Suddenly Cupid didn't know if she could go through

it alone. Not without him. She was strong and resilient, but when she coupled her strength with his, she felt indomitable, able to achieve anything. He made her whole, alive, aware.

The bare-bones truth was that she would love Burke forever, even if she couldn't live with him. Even if she had to go on with her life without him.

It would always grieve her to know she had never truly been in his heart.

Another pain hit her. "Me?" she said, pinching off the word. "I'm going to the hospital. To have our baby. Did you want to come?"

Burke glanced at her. "You were going to leave me, weren't you?"

Cupid held her stomach, vaguely thinking that a bloated woman holding a watermelon was not a particularly attractive sight. "The thought crossed my mind."

When he didn't answer, or express any regret, Cupid put her head back against the seat and closed her eyes. They drove another mile in silence.

"Cupid? I didn't mean to drive you away," he said simply.

She snorted wryly, never opening her eyes. "I know. There wasn't enough time. You had to drive me to the hospital instead. For the baby you don't want."

"I never said that," he declared. "It came as a surprise, that's all."

"You knew we were having a baby, Burke. You were there from the beginning, and you should have known there were no guarantees. Not over boys or girls or—"

He sighed, heavily. "Okay. Call me dumb as a fencepost in that department. I figured from the beginning it was going to be a boy. I know how to do the boy things—the riding, the ranching, the roping. It ought to be pretty clear to you that I don't know much about the girl things at all."

Cupid opened one eye, purposely allowing it to slide in his direction.

"I grew up with men, with guy things." Burke shrugged. "It's what I'm familiar with. That doesn't mean I'm disappointed that we're having a girl. Just a little...scared."

Both of Cupid's eyes popped wide open, and she straightened, as best she could, in the seat. "You? Burke Riley? Scared?"

"Hell," he blustered. "There's a lot of things I'm scared of."

"Name one."

His jaw clenched and the muscle along his temple throbbed. "I'm scared we're not going to agree on a girl's name."

"Cute, but it's not going to get you off the hook."

"Look. I'm not disappointed about having a girl, Cupid. I'll learn. And if she's anything like you..."

"Yes?"

He hesitated. "I'll be pretty damn grateful."

Cupid winced, even as tears pricked her eyes. Grateful. That was as close as he could come to saying the words she wanted—no, needed—to hear. She'd end up like her Aunt Sirena all over again, waiting a lifetime for the man she loved to feel the same.

"Guess I figured," he continued, oblivious to her dilemma, "that if I set my mind to it, thinking the baby would be a boy, it would. I never thought beyond that."

"At least we share the same fault," she said, taking another deep breath as a strong contraction hit. She waited until it subsided. "Because I thought...if I set my mind to loving you, that someday you'd love me back."

Burke froze as if someone had smacked him with a dash of cold water.

"But what I discovered," she added, "is that it doesn't work that way for me. All my life, I've believed in love. I grew up believing that love made the world go 'round. I committed my life to introducing people to each other. It was what I did," she said carefully, "like a hobby or something."

"We need to find you a new activity," he muttered, turning in at the hospital entrance.

"You can't, Burke. Because it's who I am. It's what I am."

Pulling into the parking space near the emergency entrance, he turned on the seat to face her.

"I'm Cupid," she said softly, lightly, "and I make matches."

Burke's gaze narrowed. "Has it ever occurred to you that you may be delusional over this Cupid thing?"

She shook her head. "'Fraid not."

"Great," he said dryly. "Other women do arts and crafts. I get one who thinks she's the power behind the play in the romance industry."

Cupid's smile was thin, patient. "I've tried, Burke. Really. But our relationship won't ever work without love. Not for me, anyway. I've lost a part of myself, and I'm not sure I'll ever get it back. I can't compromise.…" Cupid gasped, as another hard contraction bore down on her.

Her body involuntarily curled into the fetal position, pressure heating her loins, her thighs. She went hot and clutched the door handle, perspiration breaking out on her upper lip.

Seeing her like that, broken in half with pain, and professing what she'd kept inside, nearest her heart, made Burke admire her strength, her commitment. She was his wife. She wasn't going to settle for second best. Not for herself. Not for him. Certainly not for their baby.

He rushed to the passenger side of the car, thinking a dozen illogical thoughts. He was scared. Scared of everything. Of having the baby. And of not having it. Of being alone, and of being together.

Of losing his heart, and of giving it away.

She couldn't compromise, and all along he'd figured a compromise was the only way out. He'd let her into his life, but just so far and not one bit further.

He was wrong. So, so wrong.

There were matters you could contain—and matters you couldn't. The tangible, like babies. The intangible, like fear and hope and desire. Or like matters of the heart.

"It's coming, Burke," she whispered, holding her breath to endure the pain.

"Breathe, Cupid," he ordered. "Pant. Like they told you."

Lifting her out, he cradled her effortlessly against his chest. She was limp and taut all at the same time. He pushed the car door shut with his hip and silently offered up a little prayer, all the while wondering if God could look down on men with hard hearts, and piecemeal emotions, and still be benevolent enough to oblige their requests.

The prayer wasn't so much for him as for Cupid. For the baby, their daughter.

Burke strode into the emergency entrance, Cupid in his arms, and stopped at the front desk. "We got a baby that's not going to wait," he announced, when the receptionist swiveled in his direction, "and a daddy that's getting mighty scared."

"Okay, now...push," the doctor ordered. "Push. C'mon."

Cupid's face, contorted from the efforts, was flushed. Burke mopped at her brow with a damp cloth with his free hand. His other hand firmly clasped hers. "You're doin' good, honey. So good," he whispered, leaning down next to her ear.

"Mmm," Cupid answered weakly, as the contraction passed. She took a long, cleansing breath. "You look so..." everyone in the delivery room stopped and gazed at her expectantly "...funny...without your cowboy hat."

Burke chuckled and tilted his head, and the surgical cap, to a rakish angle. "Who'd have ever thought I'd be wearing surgical scrubs?"

Cupid never answered, for another contraction circled her middle, cutting off her breath.

"Roll with it," Burke encouraged, putting his arm behind her back and lifting her. "We're almost there."

"Head's out," the doctor announced. "And would you look at that red hair!" Everyone, including Burke and Cupid, laughed. "A couple more, and we'll have us a baby."

The doctor guided the baby's shoulders out on the next contraction, but it took a third before the baby slipped into their world.

"You have a girl! And she looks perfect to me!"

Burke broke into a wide smile. Cupid fell back against the pillows.

A brief flurry of activity ensued as the baby was suctioned and wrapped in a warm towel, before being placed on Cupid's tummy.

She strained to look at her squalling baby. "Hey," Burke whispered, wondrously skimming a finger over the back of the baby's hand, "look at that. These hands were meant for a pair of reins. Why, I think you gave me a barrel racer."

Cupid smiled, imagining this child growing up on Burke's ranch. She could see pigtails and patched jeans, and a straw cowboy hat. She could see the split rail fence behind the house...but she couldn't see Burke. "She's so perfect," Cupid said, her voice trembling with awe and emotion.

Burke wiped tendrils of Cupid's damp hair away from her temple, then brushed her forehead with a kiss. "Like her mama," he confirmed, "perfect."

"We need to get you settled in recovery," a nurse advised, cutting in on their first moments together. "We'll get the baby cleaned up and weighed, and then bring her in. Has she got a name?"

"Pandora," Cupid answered without hesitation. "For my mother."

The nurse looked somewhat surprised at the uncommon name. But Burke just nodded.

"Pandora what?" the nurse persisted.

"Althea. Pandora Althea," Cupid announced. She slipped her hand back into Burke's, and whispered, "It's Greek. It means 'love makes all things right, for it heals the sorrows of the heart.'"

Burke grinned, then looked at the stupefied nurse, saying, "Kind of a far cry from James Robert, isn't it?"

She laughed and whisked the baby away.

"I don't know what made me think we were having

a boy," Burke said, his voice apologetic as he leaned close to Cupid's bed in recovery.

"Maybe because you wanted one?" Cupid suggested.

"Nah. I figured that's what it would be. Heck, that's all we ever had in my family. Boys. Both for my old man and his before him."

"I guess we're changing things, you and me," Cupid said softly. She ached to reach for Burke, but refused to give in to the impulse. She knew, intuitively, that the reconciliation was up to him.

"Yeah. Yeah, I guess so." Silence slipped away, and the cold stark walls seemed to echo with the discomfort they felt with each other. "But I don't care," Burke suddenly declared, hovering closer. "I don't care one whit that we don't have a boy. Honestly."

Cupid hesitated. "I believe you, Burke. But—there's other things...."

"About us?"

"What else?" Cupid smiled sadly. "We've had our fair share of differences these past months."

"Forget it, all of it," he said gruffly. "It's that new-lywed adjustment stuff. It's part of figuring out who takes out the garbage, or deciding who sleeps on which side of the bed."

"That's the easy part, Burke."

"How about...saying the wrong thing when you can't find it in yourself to say what you really mean?"

"Oh. Something like...?"

His mouth momentarily pinched at the corners. "Like...coming right out and saying I don't want to lose you," he said finally, a soft, sandpaper-like edge to his voice. "Like saying I don't mean to drive you away..." Cupid stared up at him, and her gaze never wavered from his. "C'mom, Cupid. You know I'm nothing more than a grizzly, grumbly old cowboy."

"You're more than that."

"No, I know I'm not much to love…and I don't know how you can manage it. How you've managed it all these months.

"It's been a trial," she admitted, a small smile playing over her lips.

"I guess I was so afraid of losing you that I kept pushing you away, figuring I'd rather do it myself, than have you do it to me. I want you to stay, Cupid, because I never felt this thing in my heart before. I think—" he hesitated, the confusion vivid behind his gray eyes, "—I think maybe it's love," he confided, "and I just didn't know it."

Cupid's eyes went red-rimmed, and sparkly, but she never shed one tear, not one. "I love you," she ventured.

He stared at her, his gaze fixed, his brow slightly furrowed. "I love you, too."

Cupid's heart hammered in her chest, her respiration increased, and a small electrical charge fired her neurons. The monitors beside the bed recorded something close to seismic activity.

"Burke," she reproved, "I'd never leave the man I love. Love is everything. Love is what makes you get up in the morning, what puts you to bed at night."

He chuckled and dragged a fingertip down her cheek, thinking of the amorous nights they had to look forward to. "I know," he said earnestly. "It's what makes life worth living."

The most incredible feeling of peace and commitment surrounded Cupid, putting her into a kind of afterglow.

Everything tingled. The fine hairs on her arms stood on end; her scalp rippled with sensation. Even her toes were abuzz. A warmth grew in her chest, radiating outward, until she felt warm all over.

Burke frowned. "Cupid?" he said. "You're kind of flushed. Well, it's not that, exactly. It's more like..." he looked over her head, and to the space near her shoulders, her arms "...like this red stuff...floating over your head—"

"Mr. Riley?" the nurse interrupted. "I have your baby."

He dragged his gaze away, to the nurse, and accepted the tiny bundle. He awkwardly shifted the baby in his arms, forgetting the aura. "Oh. My. Real little critter, isn't she?"

"Seven pounds two ounces," the nurse said. "Twenty inches long."

"And the reddest hair," he said absently, stroking the baby-soft down, unaware the nurse had left. He adjusted the blanket, and when he did Pandora's tiny T-shirt buckled, exposing the clear, pink skin of her shoulder, her chest. "I swear, Pandy, if you're not the mirror image of Cupid, and—"

Burke stopped. His jaw went slack and his eyebrows lifted. He looked from the baby to her mother, then back again. He lay the baby along the length of his arm, cupping her head as he inched a forefinger under her T-shirt. "Cupid? Does this thing...*this Cupid thing*," he revised, "run in the family?"

"Why?"

He tipped the baby for her inspection. "Because I swear to God I saw stars in her eyes for a moment. And she's got your sweet spot. Your birthmark. Right here. Same place, same shape, same color."

Cupid took the baby from him, her eyes widening in feigned surprise. "Oh, look at that. You're right. She does." She held the baby in the crook of her arm, protectively covering her birthmark with the receiving blanket. "Odd. You never know what you're going to hand down from generation to generation, do you?"

Burke rocked back on his heels as a glint of suspicion marked his features. He looked over her head, to where the aura had been. He glanced at the blank monitor, the one the nurse had dismissed as being "on the fritz."

"Cupid," he said thoughtfully, "you know that doctor? The one we had?"

Um-hmm?" Cupid was busy inspecting the baby's ears.

"He's single."

"Really?"

"I heard him say something about getting really tired of going home to an empty apartment. That's why he works nights."

Cupid frowned, obviously distracted. "He said that?"

Burke nodded, but Cupid never looked away from the baby to see the gesture. "Shame, isn't it?" he commented. "He really ought to meet that nurse in emergency. The one that admitted you? I got the impression she's..." he lifted one shoulder "...oh, I don't know, maybe a little lonely."

"Really?" Cupid thoroughly examined Pandora's dimpled hands.

"Do me a favor," he said, his gaze narrowing perceptively. "Introduce them."

Cupid, who had started to unwrap the baby's feet, paused in surprise. "I thought you didn't want me to do that anymore."

He lifted a shoulder. "Maybe I was wrong. About your hobbies and all."

"Mrs. Riley?" a lovely young woman inquired, poking her head in the door. "They said I could come in and check on you. You were so far along in your labor, and I was worried about you. My name's Kathleen Morehouse, and I admitted you in emergency earlier this afternoon. You may not remember me."

"Come on in," Burke invited, pausing to explain to Cupid, "This is the young lady I was just telling you about. The nurse in emergency?" He smiled a bit smugly at Kathleen. "Take a peek. We've got a healthy little girl."

"Oohh," Kathleen crooned, peering at the baby, "how precious. And look at that red hair!"

"He says she looks like me." Cupid grinned.

Cupid's doctor, Alex Whitman, thirtyish and endearingly rumpled, walked in behind the nurse. "How's our baby?" he asked, coming to stand at the end of the bed.

"Beautiful," Burke said.

"Perfect," Cupid replied.

"Great. Well, folks, I wanted to tell you I'm taking off, but I'll come in and check on you tomorrow. Things couldn't have gone better as far as I'm concerned. You get a good night's sleep and…" His gaze drifted over to Kathleen, who was tucking the receiving blanket back around the baby's toes.

"Cupid…?" Burke prompted, his head tilting in the doctor's direction as his eyes slid toward Kathleen.

"Thank you, Doctor," Cupid said, her arms tightening protectively around her baby. No matter what happened, she'd always have Pandora. And her husband. It looked like, from here on out, they came as a package deal.

A sudden vision whipped through Cupid's head. Of a doctor coming home to a houseful of children, and a woman, a nurse, who had happily given up her career to tend boo-boos with bandages.

"Doctor," Cupid said, her voice drifting into a soft, mesmerizing cadence, "this is Kathleen Morehouse. Kathleen works in emergency. Kathleen," she said carefully, measuring her words, "this is Dr. Alex Whitman."

Their gazes drifted toward each other, then locked and held. A small, slow smile touched Kathleen's lips, but Alex's lips parted and he sighed, ever so slightly.

*Ping! Just like that! Just like the old times.*

Both seemed to forget that Cupid or Burke—or even the new baby—were in the room.

Cupid settled back against the mattress and cuddled her squirming infant. Burke watched in fascination at the unfolding scenario.

"I was just going to my car," Alex said, checking his watch. "Your shift must be over. Can I walk you out?"

"I'd appreciate the thoughtfulness," Kathleen answered. "You know, I do have a few questions about admitting obstetrical patients. You could answer them for me."

They strolled out of the room, deep in conversation.

Burke stared after them. "I'll be switched."

"What?" Cupid prompted.

"You know what. You did it again."

A faint smile played on her lips, and then she chuckled, and laughed and finally, she held the baby close against her breast, her face illuminated with joy. Sheer joy.

She caught his hand, wiggling her fingers into his palm. "Sometimes you just gotta believe, Burke."

"You're back at it again, aren't you?"

She laughed.

"You did it for Moira, and what's-his-name, the hardware guy. And those two in the casino…" The realization fell into place faster than the numbers on a slot machine. "You make people happy."

"I try to."

"You're Cupid," he said, a bit of accusation in his voice. "And you make them fall in love."

"Yes," she whispered deliciously, "I do. But it's more than a hobby. Better get used to it, Burke. From here on out, we're going to be invited to a lot of weddings."

He snorted, then he threw back his head and roared.

The baby startled and Burke quieted, half afraid he'd be the cause of her wailing.

"A lot of weddings, huh? And babies, too, I suppose?"

"One follows the other, as you can see."

"Mmm."

She waited, admiring the baby, thanking her stars, her fates, that life, and Burke Riley, had intervened. "I needed your love, Burke. To thrive. To make others happy."

"And I need you, to be the Cupid in my life, to make me learn how to love. To learn how to feel it, and say it." He worked his mouth experimentally, silently, then, "I love you, Cupid."

"I love you, too."

"Love's been a long time gone, Cupid. But I'm finding my way back to it. With you."

\* \* \* \* \*

**Silhouette Books**

is delighted to present
two powerful men, each of whom is
used to having everything

*On His Terms*

Robert Duncan in
## LOVING EVANGELINE
by *New York Times* bestselling author
***Linda Howard***

and

Dr. Luke Trahern in
## ONE MORE CHANCE
an original story by
***Allison Leigh***

*Available this February wherever Silhouette books are sold.*

SILHOUETTE *Romance*

# COMING NEXT MONTH

**#1648  HER SECRET CHILDREN—Judith McWilliams**
How could a woman who'd never been pregnant have twins living in
England? Vicky Sutton was determined to discover just who had
stolen her eggs—but never expected to meet James Thayer, father of
the twins and a man afraid of parenthood! Would this twosome
become a foursome?

**#1649  PROTECTING THE PRINCESS—Patricia Forsythe**
American security expert Reeve Stratton came to Inbourg to guard
the beautiful and stubborn Princess Anya and her young son. But
close quarters with the enchanting princess was leading to some
very unprofessional ideas…and to a few stolen kisses….

**#1650  THE TYCOON'S DOUBLE TROUBLE—Susan Meier**
*Daycare Dads*
Policewoman Sadie Evans's temporary job of baby-sitting billion-
aire Troy Cramer's wayward twins was throwing her life in an
uproar. Still, it was hard to resist a man with blue eyes, broad
shoulders and a need for her that went beyond what either of them
expected….

**#1651  KISS ME, KAITLYN—Cynthia Rutledge**
Aspiring designer Kaitlyn Killeen could not afford to fall in love
with rugged Clay McCashlin—no matter how breathless he made
her feel! But the handsome rebel had a hidden agenda—and identity. Soon Kaitlyn had to choose between the career she'd always
wanted, and the enigmatic man who left her wanting more!

**#1652  IN THE SHEIKH'S ARMS—Sue Swift**
During a morning ride, the independent Cami Ellison met
Rayhan ibn-Malik, her mysterious and handsome neighbor. Caught
up in his passionate kisses, she became his bride—not realizing
revenge was in his heart. But would Ray's plan to whisk the young
beauty away to a foreign land prove that *love*—not vengeance—
was his motivation?

**#1653  A DAY LATE AND A BRIDE SHORT—Holly Jacobs**
Attorney Elias Donovan needed a wife in order to be considered
for partnership in his firm. What he ended up with was fiancée-of-
convenience Sarah Madison. Soon Sarah found herself planning
her own elaborate fake wedding! But would their time together
lead to real marriage?

SRCNM0203